thresholds

THE WALSH FAMILY

KATE CANTERBARY

VESPER PRESS

'Twas the weekend before Christmas, when all through the
North End
Not a Walsh had his life together, not even his friends;

The parties were planned by the foodies with care,
In hopes that Wes and Erin would soon find their way there;

The men were stressing over last minute shopping lists and
plans,
While the ladies were busy with work and nesting and finding
the right paella pans;

When out in the dining room there arose such a clatter,
The Halsted dogs sprang from their beds to see what was the
matter;

They whistled and shouted and called each other names,
While the secrets and announcements and surprises quickly
came;

So onto another adventure they flew
With the sleigh full of Walshes, and the Commodore too--

As they continued arguing and clamoring around,
Down the road an unexpected visitor came with a bound;

But it wasn't long until couples were all nestled snug in their beds,
With new memories of steamy holiday nights dancing in their heads.

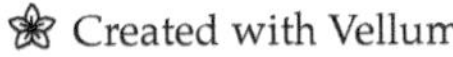 Created with Vellum

For the pervy girls.

Happy, happy holidays!

WHAT A YEAR IT HAS BEEN. The Commodore and I have had the pleasure of visiting nine countries and logging more than ten thousand miles in the RV, and spent wonderful hours with our children and granddaughter. We couldn't ask for more.

We hit the road last February with a four-month-long tour of Oceania and Asia. We visited the Australian Outback, which reminded Bill of his west Texas roots, save for the kangaroos and dingoes. The Aboriginal culture is fascinating, and we loved exploring Uluru, or Ayers Rock.

Since we couldn't agree on all things, we each indulged our own interests when we reached the coast: Bill got in plenty of surfing at Bondi Beach and I swam with platypuses. We traveled by catamaran out on the Great Barrier Reef and took in some snorkeling. I haven't yet mastered the art of underwater photography but I did get a few blurry snaps of the incredible ocean life.

From there, we headed to Tasmania. Bill and I had plenty of good laughs during this leg of our journey as Wesley's childhood nickname was always the Tasmanian Devil. All jokes aside, this southern island state of Australia is tranquil and stunning. Nearly one-third of the island is designated as national park land, and Bill and I loved hiking the Cradle Mountain reserve. We even visited a real Tasmanian Devil. Surprisingly, he had a much tamer temperament than Wesley as a toddler.

Our journey then took us to New Zealand, Fiji, Thailand, South Korea, and Japan. We spent the late summer and fall on an expedition that originated back home in San Diego and ended in Yarmouth, Nova Scotia. We followed the Pacific Coast Highway north to the Olympic National Forest, and then started our Canadian trek in Vancouver. We headed east from there, and loved every mile of it. While we're no strangers to Canada, we timed this tour to maximize the changing seasons. Bill says I took too many photos on this voyage, but I don't think such a thing exists.

But enough about us and our travels!

We're thrilled to report the continued success of Will's private security venture with his BUD/S friend Jordan. We always knew they'd make an unstoppable team, and we couldn't be more proud of the important work they're doing. Our brilliant daughter-in-law Shannon recently closed the year's largest residential property sale in Boston, and that's on top of all her other record sales. Will is lucky to be married to such a smart lady!

Wesley continues to serve as a cultural liaison to several Eastern European nations. His work with the State Department is very fast-paced and demanding, and crucial to preserving centuries of art, history, and tradition. The stakes are high and there's a lot on the line, though Wesley is uniquely suited for this role with his fluency in multiple languages and diplomatic skill. He doesn't get home nearly as much as we'd like, but he's finally putting that anthropology degree to good use!

Lauren's school kicked off its fourth year this past September, and she now has students in grades kindergarten through three. Bill and I have visited each year since the doors opened, and every time we're there, we're amazed that our little Lolo dreamed it all up and brought it to life. She's in her element and she's doing remarkable things with those children. Our son-in-law Matthew was nominated for a prestigious historical preservation prize for his renovation of a two-hundred-year-old home in Boston. It's quite the honor! If Bill and I had fifteen million dollars lying around, we'd jump at the chance to live in a Matthew Walsh signature home!

Now we're headed to New England for the holiday season. If you know Bill, you know he lovingly refers to it as pie season! We're looking forward to celebrating our precious granddaughter's first birthday and spoiling her rotten. She'll be a big sister soon, and we can't wait to welcome the newest Halsted baby into the family in January. We plan on spoiling that one, too!

Bill and I will reprise our roles as grandparent-nursemaids come Baby Halsted's arrival, and we'll remain in New England until March. At that point, we'll head out for another fabulous journey. Bill is angling for Central America and sunshine, though I love the Sierra Nevadas and springtime snow. Maybe we'll catch a bit of both!

Wishing you a holiday season filled with love and blessings,
Judy and the Commodore

"YOU'VE GOT THIS UNDER CONTROL?" Jordan asked. "You're sure?"

I rolled my eyes at the videoconference camera. My business partner had asked some version of this question five different ways in the past thirty minutes. He was tucked into his office at our Maryland training facility rather than his usual base of operations in Montauk. A team of new field agents was engaged in a final round of pre-dawn extraction and exfiltration exercises before breaking for the holidays, and he was on site to observe them in action.

"Is there something you're not telling me?" I asked. "Aside from standard protection details, we don't have any active ops next week. Are you expecting the world to fall apart over Christmas? Is there terrorist sect chatter I don't know about? A coup in the works? You're always keeping that shit from me."

"No," he said with a shrug. "But I don't want to take off for the holiday and leave you high and dry, especially with the baby coming ashore any day now."

"You make childbirth sound like guerilla warfare."

"Isn't it?" he asked with a laugh.

I considered this, and the all-too-vivid memories of Shannon promising to castrate me the last time she was in labor. She was specific about it, too. She was going to cut off my balls and hang them from a tree in the backyard.

Oh, but I loved that crazy woman. It was hard to believe that Froggie was thirteen months old and eagerly awaiting the arrival of her new brother or sister. I was convinced Shannon was carrying a girl. She was convinced I was wrong. Nothing new there.

"Somewhat," I conceded. "But that's not the point."

"Maybe we should put Shaw in charge again. He'd didn't fuck anything up last month." Jordan ran his knuckles over his chin. "We'll both take the holidays off. You'll have a baby, I'll have a vacation, and Shaw will do the work."

Annoyed, I leaned back in my chair and folded my arms over my chest. We'd established this plan months ago. Jordan's deputy, Jeremy Shaw, had managed the office and our operatives over the Thanksgiving holiday. I was on call for Christmas and Jordan was taking New Year's. It was written down, scheduled up, done. I was a fan of calling an audible when the situation warranted it, but this wasn't one of those situations.

"Dude." I glared at him through the screen. "I have shit to do. I'm not going to dick around with you all day."

Jordan busied himself by shuffling papers and jerking his shoulder as if any of that explained our meeting's strange detour. He tapped a file on his desk several times before meeting my gaze.

"I'd rather pull Shaw than risk this baby storming the

beaches early." He shrugged. "I'm scheduled to talk to Shaw soon," he said. "I'll run it by him. He doesn't have a personal life, so I'm sure it's fine."

I yanked off my ball cap and ran my fingers through my hair before glancing back at Jordan. "Just for saying that, this kid will take her sweet time getting here. I told you about all the times we went in for scans and she wouldn't cooperate."

"Yeah, and I still don't understand how it's possible," he replied. "It's not like Shannon is the wardrobe to Narnia."

"Trust me." I rolled the sleeves of my all-weather running shirt to my elbows. "It means my house is going to be filled with strong-willed women."

"Better you than me," Jordan muttered. "Listen, dude. I have a feeling. I have a sense about this. Shaw needs to cover the controls because that baby of yours is coming early."

"You have a feeling. Isn't that pleasant." I rolled my eyes. "We went in for Shannon's thirty-seven week check yesterday. The doc said she looked great and the baby was as snug as a bug in there."

"That's another thing I don't understand," he said, exasperated. "Why is everything in weeks? One of April's clients has a ten-week-old baby. What is that? Why isn't it 'baby' and then one-year-old, two-year-old, like normal life?"

"Because having a baby isn't normal life," I replied with more rueful laughter than Jordan could understand.

"All right. I have a packed schedule, and I need to do some shopping for April this afternoon without her noticing. Let's get back on track."

"You're planning to evade a covert agent trained by the world's top spy units?" I asked. Jordan met his girlfriend April after she was hired to track him. That operation went sideways when they fell into bed together, but they were on the same team now. "Better you than me."

"I'm going to try," he scoffed.

"When are you going to marry that woman?"

"You sound like my mother," Jordan grumbled.

"Mama Trish is a smart lady," I replied.

"Yeah, and she's hammering me about locking things down with April, too," he said. "Y'all seem to forget I've known her for only four fucking months. Y'all are crazy."

"What, like that's not enough time to know when you've found the right girl?" I asked, incredulous. "She's stabbed you, stole intelligence for you, and bested every one of our operatives in hand-to-hand combat. By my count, Cupcake vonRebound is damn near perfect."

Jordan blew out a breath. "Why is this your concern?"

"Good women get away. They don't like waiting around. They find douchey guys who wear pleated trousers and striped shirts with printed ties. They let those douchelords take them for seafood when they don't even like seafood." I nodded repeatedly. "When you find a good woman, you get a ring on her finger and you marry her as fast as she'll let you."

"Pleated trousers," Jordan said slowly. "And striped shirts and seafood." He blinked at me. "Is that the Asshole Hipster Ghost of Christmas Future? Or am I missing your convoluted point altogether?"

"The details don't matter." I pointed at him. "Come on, man. You're not getting any younger."

He flipped me off. "Thank you for that reminder."

"Anytime," I replied. I glanced down at my notes and then back up at him. "Did you ever decide which team you're taking to Jamaica with you?"

He nodded as he took a sip from his water bottle. "Just my

mother's usual security detail," he answered. "She tolerates them well enough, but she hasn't told her boyfriend Marco about them. I haven't decided what I think about that yet."

"Is it a problem?" I asked. "Based on what you've told me, the guy's decent but dumber than a bag of sand."

Jordan shook his head, his eyes wide. "I don't know what my mother sees in him. I can't figure it out."

I chuckled. "I can think of an explanation."

He shot me a thunderous glare. "Don't," he warned.

"Maybe Marco's packing some heat," I said. "Maybe he's got moves."

"If you're going to continue down this path, you should know I've had obscene dreams about your mother. Dreams, plural. They were frequent and detailed, and I'll be honest with you, Halsted, your mom's a freak."

"Yeah, it's probably the dick," I continued, ignoring him. "She's allowed a boy toy, isn't she? I hope her room is on the opposite side of the resort. You wouldn't want her and Marco keeping you up all night long."

He pressed his fist to his lips. "I'm throwing up in my mouth right now, Halsted," he choked out. "Maybe I should tell your wife about her security details."

I leaned forward, folding my arms on the desk. "Go right ahead," I replied. "I'd love it if she could aim some of that fierce third trimester energy at me instead of everyone else. Hell, I'd be *happy* if she'd just stop going to the office every goddamn day or moving furniture on her own."

He blinked down at his desk before looking back to me. "I wouldn't be able to tell April that she wasn't allowed to do anything. She'd just stab me again, or knock me on my ass," he mused.

I tried—failed—to withhold a snicker. It didn't matter that

Jordan had seven inches and one hundred pounds on April, that woman could take him any day of the week.

"I don't even know if she wants kids," he continued.

"Ask her," I said simply, "and then put a ring on that finger."

Jordan stared off into the distance as he ran his knuckles along his jaw. "I will blame you if this goes bad," he murmured.

"Of course you will," I said. "You blame me every time you're out of fuckin' paper clips, Kaisall. You'll absolutely blame me if you botch a proposal to a highly marry-able woman."

"You know what? Fuck you," he said. "I'm gonna watch April kick a former Green Beret's ass, then I'm getting on my plane with her and going to the Goldeneye resort. Don't call me until the new year, unless it's to tell me I was right and the baby came early and you've named it Jordan in my honor."

"Say hi to Mama Trish for me," I said. "Try not to kill her boy toy while you're in Jamaica. She'd be real sad about that."

"Merry fucking Christmas, Halsted," he shouted, a laugh creeping into his words.

AFTER WRAPPING up my call with Jordan, I pushed away from my desk. My work schedule was light today, and that was good news because I had a long list of other problems to solve.

I headed down the stairs from my third floor office and toward our bedroom. It was early yet, and the house was quiet. I peeked inside, pleased when I found Shannon asleep.

She was up late last night as she had a million things on her mind and couldn't rest until she got them all out. That, and the baby was kicking the shit out of her ribs.

Shannon was going to the office this morning—damn stubborn woman—but I needed that time to get a few projects under control while she was out of the house. Come four o'clock this afternoon, Walsh Associates was shutting down for the holidays and my wife was officially on maternity leave. Finally. No more driving all over the fucking universe, no more visiting goddamn construction sites, no more refereeing her dumbass brothers all day, every day. She was out of the office and her deputy Tom was responsible for her workload.

That didn't mean she was going to take it easy before the baby arrived. Why the hell would she do that?

She was determined to buy several more investment properties to "keep the boys busy" while she was out of the office. There were lists, work plans, budgets. It was enough for three years, let alone the three months until she planned to return to her regular schedule.

And that was on top of repeatedly reorganizing every piece of newborn clothing and linens, rearranging the nursery, repacking her hospital bag. Shannon was in deep with the nesting, and I had no hope of yanking her out. I could only demand she provide me with marching orders and let me do the work for her. That approach often involved us yelling at each other for an extended period of time but it was a good distraction from all the things she thought she needed to do before we met the baby.

I closed the door behind me and crossed the hall to Abby's room. We'd moved her in there and out of the nursery shortly after her birthday last month, and I still got a pang in my chest seeing her in the "big girl room." As far as I was concerned, she could be a big girl when she was forty-two and gainfully employed as a nun. There was no point between now and then in which she could be anything other than my little Froggie.

She was sound asleep in the position I'd named the Drunken Sailor—flat on her back, arms and legs flailed out, head full of wild blonde curls all over the place, drool spilling over her chin. This kid. I had no idea I could adore one little person this much.

Because she could go from Drunken Sailor to Screeching Attack Ninja in five seconds flat, I backed out of the room slowly and closed the door with more care than I gave to defusing actual bombs.

I went in search of coffee and found my father in the kitchen. The dogs weaved between his legs, each vying for more head scratches and pats. From the look of his layers and the leashes tucked into his back pocket, I'd guess they were coming in from a walk on the beach.

"Morning," I called.

"Morning," he echoed. "I'm going to get these guys set up with some breakfast. We had a nice run, didn't we, boys?"

He accepted their tail wagging as agreement and led them into the space that served as our laundry room, pantry, and canine living quarters. He returned a few minutes later and busied himself with preparing a bowl of oatmeal.

I set a pair of mugs, a jar of cold brew coffee, and a jug of milk on the countertop beside my father. "I take it you and Judy had a pleasant evening," I said as I filled my cup.

He shot me a quick glance from the corner of his eye. Yeah. He knew. He knew exactly what I was talking about. "Yes, pleasant," he replied. "Your mother enjoys watching that singing competition program. She missed it while we were overseas."

"Singing competition. Mmhmm." Keeping my eyes on him, I returned the milk and coffee to the refrigerator. "I'm sure it was the *singing competition* that woke Abby around midnight."

My father had the decency to look contrite, though I wasn't certain I'd observed that reaction from him before this moment. That was how it went with old-school SEALs like him.

"I'll make sure your mother turns it down," he said.

He collected the mug I'd left for him and carried it to the coffee pot. He must've turned it on before he went out with the dogs. Cold brew wasn't his preference, definitely not in the winter. My father was devout when it came to the hot drinks during cold weather, cold drinks during hot weather paradigm.

"The singing competition? Or the headboard banging?" He choked on his coffee, and nearly upended it as he coughed. I relieved him of the mug and gave him a firm smack on the back to clear his airway. "Are you gonna make it, or are you gonna let some fair-trade coffee take you down?"

"I'm fine, I'm fine," he said, waving me off. "I wasn't expecting that comment, that's all."

"I wasn't expecting the headboard banging."

"Don't think you can take that tone of voice with me," he snapped. "I don't care how old you are, you don't talk about your mother that—"

"Believe me," I said, cutting him off, "I'm just as unhappy about this conversation as you are." I shook my head to banish all thoughts of my parents having sex. In my house. Multiple times. Loudly. "And don't correct me if I'm wrong but I believe you had a role in last evening's activities."

We stared at each other for the longest, most physically uncomfortable moment of my life. Then my father nodded once and turned his attention back to his breakfast. He stood there, one hand in his pocket, the other on his coffee, gazing out the window at the choppy blue-gray waters of the Atlantic Ocean.

Determining that the discussion portion of this confrontation was complete, I grabbed a loaf of bread and set a few slices to toast. I didn't understand pregnancy cravings beyond my basic obligation to fulfill them, but it was curious how they varied with each baby. This time around, Shannon was obsessed with hot, spicy foods…and toast. She couldn't function without two pieces first thing in the morning.

Early on, around her third or fourth month, she left for the office with the plan of grabbing something to eat at the bakery café near Walsh Associates. She didn't even make it out of the driveway before deciding she needed some toast for the ride.

Now I fired up the oven right after looking over the night's situation reports and delivered her first breakfast straight to the bedroom.

"Rise and shine, mama," I said, jogging in place beside the bed. "There are five miles of sand with your name on them. Up and at 'em."

Shannon stretched her arms over her head, and the bedsheets fell away, revealing her round belly and tiny sleep shorts. It didn't matter whether she wore a close-fitting camisole or baggy t-shirt, she always woke up with her tummy exposed. "Do I look like I'm interested in running five miles with you?"

"You'd rather hit a spin class? What about some barre? I can dig my leotard out of the closet," I replied, still jogging. "Come on, girl. Rally."

I stopped when she beckoned me closer, and I dropped my hands to either side of her hips. She was warm and drowsy, her hair spread over the pillow like a sunrise. I adored this unpolished version of her, the one that existed only inside the four walls of our bedroom. The one reserved for me.

"Listen carefully, Commando." She closed her fingers around my shirt and tugged me down. She smiled, but it was one of her *I hope you enjoy the torture I'm about to inflict* smiles. "I've figured out what you can get me for Christmas."

"And what would that be?"

"A vasectomy," she replied. "For you, of course. But mostly for me."

I barked out a laugh. "You don't mean that," I said.

"Oh, but I do," she said, coasting her hands up my back. "You did this to me."

"I did," I said, dragging my fingers along her waist and over her belly. "Though I recall you enjoyed it at the time."

"Lies," she murmured. "All lies." She sucked in a breath then let out a low groan. "Someone's awake."

Based on the movement under my hand, this kid was doing jumping jacks in there. "I want you to stay here today."

She sighed, shaking her head. "I have a full day."

"I want you to stay here today," I repeated. "Anything you need to do, you can do from home." I tipped my chin toward her. "Save the eye rolling. That shit doesn't work on me."

"Will, I'm fine, and I need to do this. I'm going to be annoyed if I can't get everything done before the holiday."

"Then Abby can stay with my parents, and I'll go in with you."

"That's not going to work. I have meetings and—"

"And I have a responsibility to take care of you," I said,

cutting her off. "I'll sit through your meetings. I'll do whatever you need and go wherever you need to go."

"Yeah, Will. Sure. You won't last ten minutes in a meeting with my brothers."

"I'll be fine," I replied. "They might end up hog-tied but that can't be helped."

"There will be no commando tactics in my office today," she said with a decisive nod. "You can drive me to the office—"

"That's a given, mama." I had to swallow a laugh. Shannon couldn't drive out of the garage with her belly. She hadn't been able to reach the steering wheel in weeks.

"I'll get one of the boys to bring me home," she continued, edging up to lean back against the pillows. "Judy promised Abby we'd decorate cookies tonight, so I'll be back for that."

"The Christmas chaos is going to break loose tonight," I warned. I handed her the toast. "The grandparents have a fuck-ton of gifts for Abby, and that's on top of the special pajamas."

"I know all about the pajamas," Shannon said. "Christmas Eve and Christmas Eve Eve. She had them custom-made because Abby is a hot potato and can't wear fleece or flannel to bed."

"That's my girl," I murmured. "She's got gifts for everyone. Judy, that is. Your siblings, their wives, Sam's kid. Even Alex. I'm telling you, she went a little overboard."

"I know all about the overboard," she replied. "We've talked about it several times. She wanted to make sure it wouldn't feel like she was trying to replace my mother."

"Does it?" When Shannon hesitated, I continued, "You can tell her, and she won't take it badly, Peanut."

"No, it doesn't feel like Judy is replacing anyone," she answered. "It's just different. It's not as if she's trying to recreate childhood memories or anything. She just doesn't like that we trade bottles of liquor in a Yankee Swap as opposed to thoughtfully selecting presents for each other. I'm pretty sure she thinks we're heathens."

"Judy likes it well enough," I said easily. "It's the Navy in her. She won't leave a sailor behind or let him be forgotten on Christmas."

Shannon considered this as she ate the toast. "Lauren once told me there were always guys from the Commodore's unit coming for Sunday dinner or visiting for the holidays. I made a pervy comment about it at the time—"

"Of course you did," I muttered.

Her eyebrow arched before she continued. "But I understand that it's Judy's way. That, and"—she giggled into her toast—"shaking the house down to the damn foundation."

"I had a talk with the Commodore this morning," I said, glancing away. "I imagine the vasectomy would be only a bit more uncomfortable than a conversation with my father about him nailing my mother."

"They've been loud before, but," Shannon started, shaking her head at the plate, "but that was intense."

"I don't need the reminder." A whole body shiver shook the thought away. "Eat. Please. Anything but that discussion."

"Do you think Wes is going to make it?" she asked, her teeth sawing over her lip.

"I don't know, Shannon. Chances are good he's stowed away on a cargo plane out of Moscow and he'll show up on our doorstep Christmas morning."

That was the truth. I had no idea where he was or why he'd missed three check-ins with his CIA handler in the past two weeks, but none of that was atypical for my brother. He took his work right to the edge, and he didn't look back. But I didn't like the circumstances of his recent silence, or the chatter Jordan and I picked up during a Ukrainian mission last week.

"I'm worried about him," Shannon said.

"Do not worry about Wes," I said. We couldn't add anything more to Shannon's stress list. "He knows what he's doing."

"I know, but I saw on the news—"

"Let me stop you right there," I interrupted. "You're not allowed to watch the news. Remember when you sent me that article about human traffickers hanging out at an Ikea?"

"Yes, because that story was insane and—"

"And I'm not fucking around when I tell you that you're not allowed to read that shit. That is the last thing you need to worry about," I said.

"You know what's wonderful?" she asked in the sweet voice that told me I was about to get my ass nailed to the wall.

"What's that, Peanut?"

"That you allow me to read at all," she replied. "You're one of the good ones, Commando."

"Thank you for recognizing that after all these years," I said. "Now, as I was saying, I don't care what you saw on the news because that kind of reporting is four thousand layers away from Wes's operation in Russia. There will not be a time when the reality of covert affairs like his will ever appear on the nightly news or front page headlines."

She considered this for a moment, nodding slowly while she nibbled her toast. "So, we'll leave a place for him at the table. There will be plenty of food, and we have the room."

If he makes it back in time.

I didn't say that. I didn't need to. I could tell from the furrow in Shannon's brow that she was thinking the same thing.

"Remind me to set up the spare room for him," she added, setting her empty plate on the side table. "I can't remember the last time those sheets were changed."

"No," I said flatly. "You're not changing sheets."

"Will, for fuck's sake, I'm not putting your brother in a questionably clean bed after he's been undercover in Russia for a short eternity," she cried. "You'd think I said I was going out back to dig up that boulder on the edge of the property or chop and stack wood."

"Please tell me those aren't actual items on your to-do list because I will lock you in this room."

"Please suck my dick."

We glared at each other for a long beat. I blinked first, and only because her breasts were screaming for my attention. With a finger curled around the strap of her camisole, I tugged it down until her nipples popped free.

"Hello, my pretties," I murmured against her skin.

"You're not going to distract me," she said as I dropped light kisses all over her chest. "Nothing is going to distract me today. I have a lot to do, you know. I'm hoping I can close sales on two of Riley's properties. It would be great to get them off the books, especially since they're such unique homes. But I haven't heard from the buyer's agent since yesterday morning. I don't know where the hell this guy went, but if I don't get a response this morning, I'm moving to backup offers. And then I'm working on something for Matt, and really hoping to finalize that today or tomorrow. Oh, and then there's a new project for Patrick. I need to move quickly on that one."

"Tomorrow's Christmas Eve, Peanut. Time to close up shop for the holidays," I said, my lips on her breast and my palm on her belly. "And this little swimmer."

"I'll close up shop when I'm ready."

"I realize you're not familiar with the notion of vacations, Shannon, but this might be the time to learn," I said. I ran my tongue over her nipple and grinned when it pulled a needy cry from her. "It will make me happy."

"When has that ever been my priority?" she asked, breathless.

I peeled off her camisole and tossed it to the floor. "There's a first time for everything, Peanut."

"Do we still have time to leave town?" she asked, grinning as she tugged my shirt off. "Maybe this is the year we make it to Mexico. If you go, I will definitely follow this time."

"Too soon, Shannon," I said, shaking my head. "Too fucking soon." I nudged her legs apart but she snapped them shut. "What?"

"There's probably a Mesozoic forest growing down there," she argued, her face twisted in a pout.

"There's not," I promised. I trailed my fingers along the smooth skin of her inner thigh as she went right on pouting. "And even if there was, I wouldn't care."

I gestured to the erection throbbing against my track pants as proof.

"Your standards need some work, Commando."

Impatient, I pulled her shorts down and tossed them aside. She didn't wear undies to bed, and that was the only gift I needed for Christmas, my birthday, our anniversary, and the Fourth of July. "My standards are exactly right," I murmured. I pressed my palm to her inner thigh, silently asking her to open for me. "Stop worrying about this, everything. Relax. You are perfect right now. Everything about you is perfect."

With a sigh, Shannon parted her legs. "If my water breaks and I go into labor, and you drown in amniotic fluid, you'll have only yourself to blame."

I glanced up at her, taking in the vinegary-sweet scowl on her face. "I'll remind you that I've survived far more harrowing experiences," I said. "I'll also remind you that I did this to you, and I can deal with the consequences." I reached up and ran my hand over the swell of her belly. "Now, let me take care of you."

Two

MATTHEW

I **WAS** on my third home design of the morning when Lauren rolled over and wrapped her arms around my waist.

"Why are you awake?" she mumbled into my side. "It's still dark out."

"That's December in Boston for you," I replied, still focused on nailing the look for this house. It was close but not there yet. I was going to get it there if it killed me. "The sun doesn't come out until seven in the morning, and it sets before four thirty."

"But you're an early bird nonetheless," Lauren said.

"I am when I have this much work on my plate," I said.

Truth be told, I hadn't been sleeping much lately. Too much on my mind. And I was going to build her that house. I was going to do it. I'd been promising her this for years now, and it had never been the right time. I couldn't think of a better time than now. Right the fuck now. Even if I stayed up all night, every night until I finished it.

"How are you feeling today?" I asked. I brushed my hand over her hair before returning to my work.

She nestled closer, her head resting on my lap and her fingers drawing lazy circles on my flank as she yawned. "No complaints."

I glanced away from my tablet to smile down at her. "That's what I like to hear."

"But I don't want to jinx it by saying that. Tiel was fine for almost four months and spent the rest of her pregnancy with crackers in one hand and antacids in the other." She levered up on her elbow to peer at the sketches on my screen. "What are you working on?"

"Just some designs," I said, not yet ready to share the details with her. I wanted this squared away and solid before I showed her anything. No half-assing it for the mother of my child.

I was still coming to terms with the fact we were going to be parents. I'd figured we'd have a couple of months of trying before anything came of it, but that wasn't how it worked with Lauren and me. Hole in one on the first shot.

If I was being quite honest, I'd admit that I was a little rattled by this. I was anxious—an emotion I didn't understand or enjoy—and edgy. I was freaking out about ridiculous things. Vitamins, doctors, statistics. None of it made me feel any better. I was driving Shannon crazy with my need to find a property. I wanted something I could tear down or fully restore, and it had to meet a long list of additional requirements. She hadn't found the right one—yet—and it was one of the many things keeping me up at night.

On top of all that, Lauren was as chill as a pickle. My listmaker, my action-planner, my over-preparer was sailing through her first trimester without breaking a sweat. She couldn't stand the smell of fish and she fell asleep on the sofa within five minutes of getting home every evening, but she was living the pregnant life as if she was made for it.

"All right, well," she started, throwing back the blankets, "I'm going to hop in the shower."

"Okay," I murmured, watching her pad into the bathroom as she rubbed her eyes. "It's not necessary to hop. Acrobatic stunts are not required."

"Good clarification," she called. "I was planning a back handspring but I'll scrap that for now."

I heard the faucet turn on and then the shower, and I stared at my tablet without seeing. The shower door opened and closed. I was being ridiculous again. I knew that. I wasn't sure whether recognizing my ridiculousness made it better or worse, or if this sort of thing even had gradations. Perhaps it was just a state of being. A condition. Just like pregnancy. You were either ridiculous or you were not.

"I am," I mumbled to myself, tossing my device to the bed and sprinting into the bathroom. "I'm totally fucking ridiculous. And it's all her fault."

I stripped off my clothes as I went, unconcerned with the sloppy trail behind me. I pried open the shower door, careful to keep the water and warm air contained, and stepped in behind her.

"Mind if I join you?" I asked.

"Um, I don't," she said, a laugh ringing in her words. "But you know I don't do shower sex on weekdays. This is a purely utilitarian shower. Leg shaving, exfoliation, all that stuff. You don't get to soap up my boobs and pretend you're being helpful. Okay?"

"That's fine," I replied, pressing my chest against her back. I kept my hands to myself to prove I was on board with her terms. "I'll just watch."

She whirled around to face me and—I couldn't help it—my hands flew to her hips. Didn't she know that the floor was slippery? If she wasn't careful, she was going to take a tumble and break her neck. If there was one thing Lauren did with consistency, it was trip over nothing.

Goddamn honed granite. What the fuck was I thinking when I installed that death trap?

"Did you get in here with me because—because you don't trust me to bathe alone?" she asked, her voice pitching higher with each word.

"Of course not," I said. "I trust you completely, and you're more than competent when it comes to bathing."

"I meant," she started, narrowing her eyes, "are you in here because you want to supervise me? And not the fun kind of sexy supervising where you tell me I've been a dirty, dirty girl, but the anxious kind where you're afraid I'm going to fall and break my neck?"

"Sexy," I said with a convincing nod. "Definitely sexy. Fun, too. But also practical because this is one of your utilitarian showers. In other words, I'll just stand here, thinking about how you've been a dirty, dirty girl, and you do your exfoliating."

She pointed at my face. "You're still nodding. I don't believe you." Her gaze dropped to my crotch and the erection pointed in her direction. "And this looks like an ulterior motive to me."

"No ulterior motives," I replied. I was aiming for relaxed. It came out like a drill sergeant's order. I blew out a breath as she rolled her eyes at me. Rolled her eyes but also palmed my dick. "I meant—it's just—*fuck*. I can't think when you do that."

"Try," she said, stroking me with long, slow pulls that made it difficult to stand, let alone form coherent words. "Harder."

"Sweetness, please. I just want to make sure you'll be okay, and I get to run my hands over your naked body. It's all good, right?"

She abandoned me and my cock, and reached for the shampoo. "I'm going to wash my hair now," she announced, squirting a dollop into her palm, "and I'm not going to talk to you. I'm going to wash my hair and enjoy my shower, and I'm not going to entertain caveman behavior this morning."

"You don't have to say anything," I replied. I turned my head while she lathered her hair but I wasn't letting go. "But turn around so I can wash your tits."

"And by *wash* you mean play with my tits while you rub your cock all over my ass," she said, ducking under the spray to rinse her hair.

Yes, that's exactly what I mean.

"I thought you weren't saying anything." I watched the soap sluicing over her skin, salivating at her body's sweet roundness. My hands found her hips, and I tugged her against me, fitting her soft against my hard.

"And I thought you understood this wasn't a sexytimes shower," she replied with a laugh.

"It's not," I said, sliding my cock between the globes of her ass as I cupped her breasts. They were fuller and heavier than they used to be, and stroked my thumbs over her nipples as I pushed inside her. "I'm being helpful."

Her hands slapped against the tiled wall. "If you think this is helpful, you've lost your damn mind, Matthew."

I slipped my hand between us and guided my cock into her wet heat. "Trust me. You'll be thanking me for this later," I said through a groan.

Three

RILEY

"THANKS FOR BREAKFAST, BABE," Alex said as she shrugged into her winter coat.

Her cheeks were rosy and her lips were turned up in an easy smile, and a patch of beard rash colored her neck. There was nothing better in the world than slow, bleary, half-asleep morning sex with the woman I loved.

I swung my messenger bag over my chest, smiling at my handiwork. "Anytime, Honeybee," I said. But then I remembered woman could not survive on cock alone. "Do you want me to grab some tacos or a burrito for you? I don't mind swinging by the hospital before my meeting."

"No worries," she replied. She checked her bag for her keys, phone, pager, and wallet, murmuring *check* as she located each one. "Hartshorn always has a stockpile of protein shakes. I'll be fine."

"I've said it before and I'll say it again: I wouldn't want to be near you and your scalpel when you've skipped a meal."

"Yeah, yeah," Alex muttered as we headed out. "I wouldn't want to be near you and your sledgehammer when you haven't consumed the right ratio of burritos, hot sauce, and coffee on a given day."

I held the door open, and then followed her into the hall. It was dark and narrow, but that was the way of brownstone buildings. If you wanted to believe in ghosts, this was the place for it. Steep, slice-of-pie stair steps, high ceilings, shadowy corners. And thin as fuck walls that told me Alex's upstairs neighbor just happened to be leaving his apartment at the same time.

"Come here." I pressed my palms against her cheeks and kissed her forehead. She offered me a quick peck on the corner of my lips—anything longer and she'd never make it to surgery on time—and leaned in while I swallowed her up in a tight embrace.

The sound of footfalls on the staircase had me sighing into Alex's hair.

"Oh. Hello."

"Stremmel," I called in reply.

I glared at him over Alex's head. I didn't like the guy. I couldn't put my finger on a decent reason other than he seemed like a miserable son of a bitch. He was new to the hospital and the city, and made a point of telling everyone how much he loathed both.

Good times.

"Hey, Sebastian," Alex said. "How's it going?"

"Well," he said, sighing, "I'm still here. That's gotta be worth something."

Alex tipped her head to the side, nodding slowly. "If that's the best we can do today," she started, "then that's the best we can do. Small victories, right?"

"Yeah," Stremmel murmured, almost to himself.

It was as though the guy didn't know how to appreciate

being alive. I didn't know where he was from or why he had such a massive hair across his ass, but he needed a major attitude adjustment. More than any of that, I didn't know why Alex was being so damn nice to him. My girl subscribed to the sink or swim school of thought, and she had no patience for boo-hooing bitches. Why she wasn't demanding that Stremmel get the fuck over himself and straighten out his priorities was a mystery to me.

And that mystery meant my patience for this bastard could fit in a shot glass.

"Are you scheduled next week?" Alex asked. "Or are you leaving town for the holidays?"

"Yeah," he repeated. "I mean, I'm here. I'm covering a few different services. Running the ER for a couple of days. That's the prize for being the new guy, apparently."

Alex glanced over her shoulder at me, and I smiled in spite of myself. I knew what she was thinking, and I wasn't happy about it.

"There's a small get-together on Christmas Eve," she started, gesturing between us, "and a bunch of us are going. Acevedo will be there with his wife, and Hartshorn, too. You should come."

He shook his head, and for once, I was on the same page with this guy. "You don't need a third wheel."

"Not a third wheel," Alex replied with a laugh. Seriously, where the fuck was my salty girl when I needed her? "It's really casual. Oh, and the food is amazing."

Stremmel glanced around as if he could find an exit hatch in the hallway. When he didn't find one, he scowled at the rug beneath his feet. "I'll get back to you on that," he said.

"I'll put you down for yes, but you can let me know if anything comes up," Alex said.

"Fantastic. It's so good that we bumped into each other like this," I said, my words drier than the Mojave. "So, so good."

"Are you on your way in for the day?" Alex asked him, waving toward the stairs.

Stremmel nodded. "Yeah," he replied. "Rounds."

"I'll walk with you," Alex said.

Before she could take a step, I closed my fingers around her arm and yanked her back. "Actually, Alexandra," I said, not bothering to finish that sentence. I wasn't surrendering my last moments of the morning with Alex to this guy.

Stremmel held up a hand as he crossed the landing and started down the stairs. "I'll catch up with you some other time," he called.

Alex whirled around to face me. "What?"

I backed her up against the wall, my knee moving between her legs and my hands landing on her waist. My lips met hers as I leaned into her, crowding every inch of her space and swallowing her surprised gasp.

"How much time," I breathed between kisses, "do you have?"

Her fingers were in my hair, fisting and pulling in every direction. I'd look like a wreck when I got to the office, but I didn't care. I was Alex's wreck.

"Not enough," she murmured against my mouth. "And we're in the hallway."

Despite the layers of winter clothing between us, I gripped her hips harder. "So what?"

"So, we're not dry humping in the hallway," she said.

"Who said anything about dry?"

I felt her laugh on my lips, and it defused some of the irrational tension brought on by Stremmel. *Some.* She pressed a hand to my chest, pushing me away, but brought her other hand to my crotch. She cupped me through my jeans, stroking just enough to make me contemplate dragging her back into the apartment and telling the world to fuck off for the day.

"I have to go," Alex said, and there was real remorse in her voice.

Nodding, I pulled her hand away from my jeans and tugged her into my arms again. It served two purposes: I liked the way she fit me, and I couldn't handle another second of dick petting if it wasn't going anywhere. "I know," I said. "Sorry about starting that."

"No apologies," she said, her head nestled on my chest. "But you don't have to paw me every time Sebastian is around."

"I just don't like the guy," I cried. "And you're so fucking nice to him. What's that about?"

Alex glanced up at me, her eyebrow arched. "He just got here, Riley. Like, five minutes ago. He doesn't know anyone, and he told me that he left behind a fucked-up situation in California." She gave me a pointed look, the kind she'd taken out back to whittle into a goddamn dagger for situations when she needed to puncture all of my internal organs in one shot. "And I was new in town not too long ago and if it hadn't been for people like Acevedo and Hartshorn, I would've been miserable, too."

Chastened, I tucked some stray wisps of hair over her ears and kissed her forehead. "Understood," I replied. "It just takes me by surprise when you're nice to people who aren't serving you food."

"Oh, would you shut up?" she snapped. "I'm nice to people all the time. I'm delightful."

I leaned forward, my forehead touching hers, and smiled. "That's my salty girl."

GROANING, I stood in the doorway to Shannon's office, coffee in one hand, bag of breakfast burritos in the other.

Sam came up beside me, offering his own groan at the cramped space before us. "You know," he started, speaking to no one in particular, "we have conference rooms."

"Three of them," Matt said from his seat against the wall. He must've arrived early to claim one of the two available chairs. That fucker. "I counted this morning. Just to be sure I hadn't imagined them."

"It's funny that you bring it up," I replied, snagging one of the milk crates stacked near the door. "Since your ass won't be branded with a diamond pattern and 'Hood Milk' tonight."

This was the last meeting before our holiday hiatus, and everyone was ready for vacation. Everyone except Shannon. She was insistent on doing *all the work* today, and wasn't setting us free until she'd accomplished everything on her mile-long agenda for this meeting.

Shannon tapped her pen against the desk in a furious rhythm. "Shall we relocate? That's only going to take ten minutes and—"

"No," wailed Tom. "We'll power through. Branded asses and all."

"Says the guy with a flight to Vancouver waiting for him," Andy murmured. She was tucked into the far corner, sitting cross-legged on the floor.

"You're damn right," he replied. "I'm getting out of town even if I have to snowshoe there."

Aside from my oldest sister, the entire crew was counting down the seconds. My brothers and I had an afternoon of shopping planned, and we were preparing for that the way any fool who left it all until the last minute should: with alcoholic fortification. The premise was beer, bourbon, and burgers, and once we'd consumed all of that, we'd set forth in search of gifts for the women who owned us.

There was only one problem with that premise as it pertained to me. Alex and I had agreed upon an impossible pact. A homemade holiday gift pact. Not only would shopping violate the terms of this pact, but I didn't know what to select for her even if I could buy something.

So, here I was, fucking up our first Christmas together. Just another day in the shambles.

"Can we begin?" Patrick asked. He was perched on the opposite side of Shannon's desk, looking as unhappy as the rest of us. "Shannon is comfortable in here. The next time you're nine months pregnant, Sam, we'll convene wherever you wish. Until then, shut the fuck up."

"Now that's a fun challenge," Tom said under his breath.

"Hey, Andy," I called, leaning over to catch her eye. "Alex invited Stremmel, that asshole who lives in Nick's old apartment, to the party tomorrow night. We saw him in the hallway this morning and I think she felt obligated." I jerked a shoulder, doing my best to express that I wasn't part of the decision-making process.

"Is Magnolia coming?" Patrick asked. "I wanted to talk to her about some projects."

"How quickly the roof garden tide turns," Sam muttered.

"No, she has family events," I said to Patrick. I shifted back to Andy. "If inviting Stremmel is a problem just say it, and I'll tell that party-crashing bastard to find his own holiday soiree somewhere—"

"Nope," she replied, flipping the pages of her notebook and marking an entry. "Nick invited the other doctor in their building, Hartshorn, so it's fine. I like Hartshorn. I just need a bigger paella pan."

"Are you ever sleeping in your bed again?" Sam asked, nudging my elbow.

"There's a new home goods shop in Kendall Square," Tom said to Andy. "Really nice selection. You might want to check that out if you're looking for top-notch authenticity."

I ignored the food nerd conversation flying between Andy and Tom, and asked Sam, "Why would I do that when I could have sex with my girlfriend instead?"

"He makes a good point," Matt said under his breath.

"We haven't seen you in a while," Sam said. "Alex is welcome at the firehouse, you know."

"Yeah but the firehouse has those obnoxious rules about not walking around naked or having sex on the kitchen table, and we like both of those things."

"We do not need to discuss this," Shannon said. "I don't want to hear anything about your bare ass on the kitchen table."

"No, we don't." I glanced over at Tom with an appreciative nod. He was beating the hell out of his keyboard and jostling his knees like the device required the kinetic energy to keep up. "That is one sharp turtleneck sweater, Thomas. Can I borrow it sometime?"

He didn't even look at me when he replied, "No."

"You know, now that I think about it, that sweater wouldn't fit me. Too small." I flexed a bicep. "Wouldn't want the guns stretching it out. Where can I get one of my own?"

His gaze still glued to his laptop screen, he blew out an exasperated breath. "If I miss my flight to Vancouver, I'll suffocate you with this sweater."

Sam snapped his fingers. "Andy, I forgot to tell you that

Tiel's friend Ellie is staying with us for the holidays," he said. "She got in yesterday morning and she's staying for a bit. A couple weeks, I think. Her band isn't touring for the next six months and she hadn't met Dave yet so—"

"Would you get to the point?" Shannon said. She was tapping her crystal-encrusted letter opener against her palm as though she meant to throw it at Sam. "I'm not going to speak for Andy but I will say a group text went out when Ellie arrived, and we all know she's here although you seem hell-bent on explaining her life to us."

After a long silence, I sang under my breath, "Have a holly, jolly Christmas. It's the best time of the year."

"As I was saying," Sam continued with more dramatic flair than necessary at this hour, "Ellie is also joining us tomorrow night."

"Okay, got it," Andy said, consulting her notes again. "Is there anyone else? Anyone at all? It's fine if you want to invite more people but I want to make sure there's enough food and drink for everyone. This is your last chance."

"We should check with Erin," Matt said.

"Erin is on a flight back from the South Pacific," Shannon snapped. "The last thing she needs right now is us bothering her with this madness."

"Deck the halls with boughs of holly," I sang. "Fa la la la la, la la la la."

"Can we get to the fucking agenda before I die of old age?" Patrick roared. "I'd like to get through the investment proper-ties and active client projects, and then confirm key dates for January."

"And I'd like to discuss the issues we've uncovered with the restoration in Bay Village," Sam added.

Matt snorted. "The foundation is out of level. It needs to be fully rebuilt, and you need all new headers. Those beams aren't supporting shit right now."

"Yeah, Jugger, I know all that. I read your damn engineering report. You did an exceptional job of identifying issues but failed to mention solutions," Sam replied. "My question is what the fuck do we do about it? The structure's seating on the property means we're basically blowing out the entire front of the house to get in there."

Matt traced his finger over his knee, forming shapes while he mumbled numbers and calculations to himself. Eventually he said, "We'll do it like the Italianate job."

"We're never letting you work on another Italianate," Andy said. "Clearly, it's corrupted you."

"Clearly," Sam agreed.

One of Matt's properties, a gorgeous but severely neglected Italianate in the South End, recently hit a major industry association's short list of best restorations this year. The honor was great, and it topped Sam and Patrick's heavy shelf of awards. It was a surprise to all of us, perhaps most of all Matt, but now he couldn't help himself.

"I think I've figured out why we're crammed in here like marlin in a sardine tin," I said, glancing around the room. "It's Matt's ego. If he left, the rest of us would be very comfortable."

"Let's try that," Patrick said, hooking his thumb over his shoulder. "Go sit in the hallway, Jugger."

"Fuck you all." Matt stood and dragged his chair to just past the doorframe. "Better?"

"So much," Andy said. A chorus of murmured agreement and nods went up.

"Can we talk solutions now? I need to straighten this out before work begins next month," Sam said.

Matt held up his hand. "At the risk of being hammered for

this, you know I'm right. I'll take care of the structural rehab specs, Sam."

"Great," Sam murmured. He shook his head as he typed. "That was only ten times more complicated than it needed to be."

"Hark! The herald angels sing," I whispered.

"Moving on," Patrick said.

"But," Matt continued, "just so we're clear, we *are* doing it like the Italianate job."

I sighed at my burrito. "Get some restraint, son."

"Who knew a little public acclaim would turn you into an asshole?" Shannon asked. She threw her pen at the desk. It skittered over the surface and bounced off Patrick's arm. If he noticed, it didn't show. After more than a decade of working alongside her, he'd probably tuned out her intermittent pen throwing. "You used to be the nice one around here."

"We're going to take away your design credits if you're going to be such a douche canoe about it," Patrick said.

"Even Riley handles good press better than this," Sam added.

"Excuse me, what?" I asked. "Are you suggesting I'm anything short of professional?"

"No, I'm not suggesting anything," Sam replied. "I'm stating it clearly."

"I take offense to that, sir," I said.

"Your jeans are unzipped," Sam said. "Come talk to me about professionalism when that's handled."

"I hear some offices have holiday potlucks," Andy mused from her spot on the floor. "We have verbal brawls and pissing contests."

"But instead of saving those events for one-off holidays,"

Shannon said, sweeping her arm out, "we do it all year. It's what sets us apart. Competitive advantage, if you will."

"I'm leaving in ten minutes, regardless of whether we're finished," Tom announced. "You should also know that, if I meet a husky Canadian with good hands and some chest hair, I won't be returning in January." He glanced up from his screen. "Good hands, chest hair, and a job."

"The holy trinity," Andy said.

"Is that all I am to you?" Patrick asked, his gaze cutting across the room at Andy.

"No," she replied, "but it's a good foundation."

"You're coming back," Shannon said, her letter opener pointed in Tom's direction. "Bring the husky Canadian home with you."

"Then we're running through the properties," Patrick said. "Get your updates ready."

"My update is that everything is fine, on budget and on track, and I'm ready to start this vacation," Sam said.

"What he said." Andy pointed her pen at Sam.

"Same," Matt echoed from the hall.

Everyone shifted to stare at me, expectant. I took my sweet time paging through my notes and sipping my coffee before responding. Like a true professional. "Yeah, I'm good."

Tom slapped his laptop shut. "I'm out," he said. "Happy Christmas. Merry Hanukkah. A joyful solstice. Pleasant tidings to all."

"Good luck finding that hairy-chested husky boy," Andy said. "I'm rooting for you."

"All right. We're done for the year," Patrick announced. "Everyone out."

"Joy to the world," I sang.

"I'M READY FOR HARD LIQUOR," Patrick said as he pulled on his coat. He'd been behind closed doors with Shannon for the past two hours while Matt, Sam, and I worked on that Bay Village restoration. More precisely, Sam worked and I smacked Matt upside the head every so often to keep him in line. "Copious amounts of it."

"Seconded," Matt called.

"Why do I have the feeling we're going to have group therapy over lunch?" Sam asked.

I stood in Matt's office, my outerwear in one hand, my phone in the other, but I was struggling. Boutiques with girly shit and sparkly things weren't going to help me in the least. While the liquid lunch sounded fantastic, it wasn't getting me any closer to solving my gift issues.

Unless I blew off the rules and went straight for an engagement ring. I'd considered that a time or twenty but it didn't feel right. I had no doubts about Alex or marrying her but this wasn't my moment.

At least, I didn't think it was my moment. I'd know, right?

"Would you rather we eat and drink in silence?" Matt asked Sam.

"Sam wouldn't make it three minutes," Patrick said to Matt. "He complains the most, and then he unloads the most baggage."

"You two are in ripe moods," Sam grumbled. He gestured to me. "What's the story here? Get yourself together. We're going to lunch." He pivoted, glancing at Matt and Patrick. "Where we'll conduct group therapy."

"I think I'm going to skip that," I replied. "I do love

unwinding your problems but I have to deal with a few of my own this afternoon."

"Which problems? You didn't raise any issues in the meeting," Patrick said. "I want to know if there are issues."

I shook my head and waved him off. "Put your worry boner away, okay?"

"Charming," Sam murmured.

"Whatever you have on deck can wait a couple of days," Matt said. He zipped up his coat and stuck his hands in the pockets. "We have a table for four. It's the special beer, bourbon, and burgers menu, too. Your favorite."

"I know, I know. It's tempting." I dropped my outerwear onto a chair, officially signaling my decision to stay at the office. "I'm not feeling like bourbon this afternoon."

Matt pointed at me. "That, gentlemen, is the look of a man freaking out about his first major gift to a woman."

Patrick rubbed his jaw as he stared at me. "Doesn't get any easier," he murmured.

"Not at all," Matt agreed.

"You two are obviously incompetent," Sam said. "There is nothing easier than shopping for Tiel."

"You are full of shit," Matt replied.

"Completely full of shit," Patrick agreed.

"If it's so easy," Matt started, "what did you get her?"

Sam crossed his arms over his chest as he glowered at them. "I haven't selected anything yet but I have several ideas in mind."

"Likely story," Patrick replied.

"Yeah, you're one merry band of motherfuckers," I said. "Maybe I'll catch up with you later."

"Text me if you change your mind," Matt said.

They shuffled out, leaving me alone in Matt's office. With

all of our support staff gone for the holiday, the building was as quiet as I'd ever heard it. Silence punctuated only by some incessant pen tapping replaced the constant hum of printers and copiers.

I rounded the corner from Matt's office to Shannon's, and knocked on her open door. "Do you have a minute?"

She waved me in, nodding, as she scribbled a note on the margin of a contract. "Why aren't you out with the boys?"

With a dramatic sigh fitting of my current circumstances, I flopped into the wingback chair in front of her desk. "Shambles, Shannon. Shambles."

"I can't wait to hear this." She hit me with an arched eyebrow but returned to her contract. "Start at the beginning."

"The boys are going shopping but I'm not *allowed* to shop. Alex and I decided we'd give each other homemade Christmas gifts," I said. "That would be fine if I could figure out what to give her."

Shannon shuffled her papers into a file folder and tapped her pen on the desk's edge. "Aren't you supposed to be the creative one here?"

"Why does that sound like an insult when you say it?"

She shifted in her chair and twisted her ponytail around her fingers. "Don't make me throw things at you."

I held up my hands, ready to block any projectiles coming my way. "Help me figure this out," I said. "I will do anything. Put me to work. I'll patch roofs and unclog drains. Fold laundry. Do your grocery shopping. Whatever you want. Just help me find a gift for Alex so I don't fuck everything up."

"I want lunch," she said, her words coming out like a dare. "I need to eat every two hours or I get nauseous."

"And I'd be happy to buy you three or four lunches to prevent anything that might involve vomit," I replied.

"I have some errands to do," she continued. Another dare.

"I'll be your chauffeur." I dropped my hands and leaned forward. "Seriously, Shannon. Give me some ideas and I'll be your slave for the day. Pretend I'm Tom, but without the sexy turtleneck."

She rubbed her belly as she considered my offer. "I'm good with sparkly gifts, Riley," she said. "I can pick out engagement rings and crystal vases. I'm not sure I can help you with home-made goods."

I flattened my hands on her desk. "You're good with gifts that are thoughtful, meaningful, and perfect. You know how to make people feel special with the right present. I just want to make her feel special and I can't figure out how to do that by myself."

She waved her hands in front of her face as she blinked. "Goddamn," she whispered. "You can't say things like that to me right now unless you want me crying all over the place." She yanked a tissue from the box and dabbed her eyes. "All right, fine. But I was serious about lunch."

"So was I," I replied, popping to my feet. "I'm a growing boy."

"MAKE HER DINNER," Shannon suggested from behind her menu. "The whole deal. Flowers, candlelight, four courses."

"That's brilliant," I said. "All I need to do is find four complementary breakfast cereals for those courses because that's the extent of my cooking capabilities."

She turned back to her menu. "Then cooking is out."

"Cooking is definitely out."

The waiter arrived at our table, and Shannon fired off a

barrage of questions about several different dishes. "Can you tell me how the bread is toasted?" she asked. "I hate when it's toasted on the griddle."

Because I loved absurd explanations as much as the next guy, I asked, "And why is that?"

"I don't like meat-flavored bread," she replied, as if it was a universal truth. "It tastes like everything that's been cooked on that griddle since the dawn of time. Bacon, cheese, eggs, onions, and—worst of all—meat. If I wanted my bread to taste like a cheeseburger with bacon and onions, I'd order that."

"It's toasted on the griddle," the server replied, the anguish obvious in his words.

Since she wasn't close to making a decision on her order, I zoned out while she fired off another round of cross-examination. I barely noticed when she finished. I was too busy growing old and weary.

"Make one of those cute little coupon books," she said after the waiter left the table. "You know what I mean. Back rubs, letting her choose the movie, that sort of thing."

I reached for the salt and pepper shakers, sliding them from hand to hand. "I suppose that could work," I said with all the reluctance in the world. "But those things aren't gifts. They're not even examples of playful compromise. They just seem like the sort of thing you do when you've been married for six years and require some handwritten vouchers to tolerate each other."

Shannon recoiled, her eyes widening. "You might be exaggerating a bit."

"Thank you for the idea," I said with as much diplomacy as I could muster. "I'll revisit it if needed."

Shannon fired off more suggestions while we waited and between bites when our lunches arrived. A mason jar of date night ideas on little slips of paper. A drive to the Berkshires. An evening of pillow fort shenanigans. A tour of Cliff Walk mansions in Newport. A movies-and-staycation weekend in the apartment.

None of them worked. They all felt juvenile or unimpressive or uninspired. This gift had to check all the boxes—except the spendy and store-bought boxes—and communicate everything. But none of them were right, and I needed something *right.*

"Make her a comic book," Shannon said as we walked back to my car after eating. "You have all those drawings of her in your notebook, in that superhero costume you invented. Take that to the next level."

"Yeah, I'd do that if I wanted to rip off Seth Cohen and *The O.C.* circa 2003," I said with a scoff. "I'd like to think I'm better than that."

"I'm not sure what you're talking about right now," Shannon said as I helped her into the passenger seat. "You might be speaking in tongues."

"Hilarious." I leaned against the open door, watching while she worked the seatbelt around her belly. "What's the next stop, Black Widow?"

"There's a sandwich shop in Cohasset I've been thinking about all week." She gave me a sheepish glance. "If you don't mind driving down there, we can stop at one of the listings I'm considering, too. Would that be okay?"

"I've never declined a sandwich," I replied. "I can't see why I'd start now."

We headed out of the city and into the glut of holiday weekend traffic, and I shifted our conversation to investment properties. We could agree on the basics there, and I knew her restoration ideas wouldn't include mason jars or a rant about meat-flavored bread.

Walking the property didn't take much time. The structure was in rough shape, and Matt was going to enjoy taking it apart and putting it back together again. But it was a storybook stone cottage with an ocean view, and we'd make a killing on a thorough restoration. I didn't know how she did it, but Shannon could pick those diamonds right out of the rough.

"We should get out of here," I said, knocking my boot against the foundation. The stone disintegrated on impact. "I can't feel my fingers or toes, this thing is a structural mess, and that path"—I pointed at the brick walkway near the front door where Shannon stood—"is uneven and getting icier by the minute. Do you have what you need?"

"I'm all set," she replied. "Sandwiches?"

"Several of them," I replied, holding out my arm to her. "In case it's not obvious, I'm happy to drive you from one eatery to another any day of the week."

"What about that?" Shannon asked. "Make Alex a list of all the restaurants you want to visit together. All she ever talks about is the great spots you two visit. It would be perfect for her. Thoughtful, too."

"The only homemade thing there is the list," I argued. "I could give her a list of destinations we should visit or places I'd like to fu—"

"Finish that sentence and you don't get a sandwich," she interrupted.

"My bad," I said. "But I don't want to give her a list. I need to do better than that."

Shannon nodded as we reached the curb. "I'll keep thinking."

"Could you?" I asked with a wry laugh. "I'm running out of

time here."

After Shannon placed a call to the realtor managing the listing to discuss an offer, she dropped her phone into the cup holder and folded her arms over her chest. "What do you think Alex is giving you?"

I shook my head as I merged into traffic. "I have no idea," I admitted.

"That doesn't help," she murmured. "What about a letter? Something flowing and heartfelt."

I snorted. "Do I look like Sam to you?"

"Weren't you telling me her bathroom needs a remodel? Why not draw up plans?"

Another snort. "Now I look like Matt?" I asked. "Regardless, that's not going to work. First, she doesn't own the apartment. I don't want to deal with extra layers of bullshit on top of the regular bullshit that comes with building on Beacon Hill. Furthermore"—I held up four fingers; it seemed like I'd made that many points—"she doesn't intend to stay in there long enough to thoroughly enjoy the benefits of that type of work."

Shannon blew out a breath, closed her eyes, and rested both hands on her belly. She winced, and I couldn't determine whether I was to blame, or the baby.

"Fine. Whatever. Don't redo the fucking bathroom. I don't care," she said eventually.

"Is everything okay over there?" I asked.

"Fine," she repeated. "But don't talk to me until there's a sandwich in my hand."

<hr>

"WHAT ABOUT A PHOTOGRAPH?" Shannon stabbed her fork at me as if she was trying to pin the idea onto my skin.

"You take enough of them—"

"Hold it right there," I interrupted. I was not prepared for this conversation. My preference for X-rated photography had no place in our second lunch. "We're not talking about my—our—*that*. We're not talking about that."

There will never be a time when my siblings didn't focus on systematically hammering me over one incident where I sent one intimate photo via group text. They'll mention it in toasts at my wedding, they'll tell stories to my children, and they'll engrave it on my tombstone.

Shannon arched an eyebrow. "I wasn't talking about *that* either. I'm just saying, I'd love a tasteful image of myself from an era before stretch marks colonized every part of my body. I'm sure Alex would appreciate a photo that represents the way you see her."

"That's not homemade." I sighed. "The photograph might've been taken at home, but I'd have to print and frame it. That would break the rules."

"Fuck the rules," she said. "I'm sure Alex isn't adhering to a literal interpretation of the agreement. I could argue that everything is, in some form, a violation of the rules."

"That's because you're a lawyer," I argued.

"You're damn right it is," she yelled, attracting the attention of everyone in this small café. "The principle gift is the photograph, and I believe it's in keeping with the spirit of the agreement."

"I know this might be hard for you to understand," I started, "but it matters to me that I do this right. I don't want to skate by on technicalities."

Shannon set her fork down and clasped her hands. "All right, I don't want to litigate this. I can accept your position even if I don't agree with it," she said. "If not a photograph, what about a drawing?"

I started to object but stopped myself. That might work. "Yeah," I murmured. "I can do that."

Shannon dragged my basket of french fries closer, plucking a few from the top. "I know you're trying to stay above board —and it's great you've decided to be a law-abiding citizen now —but put it in a cute frame. It doesn't have to be big or ostentatious. Just something lovely she can keep in her bedroom."

I shrugged. "That does sound nice," I said. "Now, where else am I taking you today?"

"Wait a second," she said, holding up her hand. "Did we solve your Christmas conundrum? Did we finally, after hundreds of rejected ideas—"

"It wasn't hundreds of ideas," I said while Shannon rolled her eyes. "Two dozen. No more than thirty."

"After *hundreds* of rejected ideas, are you choosing this one? We've found the one gift that meets all your requirements?"

"One gift to rule them all," I said darkly.

Ignoring that prime *Lord of the Rings* reference, Shannon continued, "You're saying yes to the drawing?"

I stared at her, unimpressed with the tirade. "Yes, Shannon. I'm certain. Thank you for your exhaustive assistance." I rolled my hand, gesturing for her to continue. "What's our next stop?"

"You're welcome." She pulled her notebook out of her bag and flipped it open. "I only have a few things to handle," she said. "You don't mind touring a property in Lexington, do you? It just came on the market, and I want to get in while I can. Oh, and I have to see a new one in Charlestown."

"Is that all?" I asked.

"I need to grab some nursing camisoles," she said. "I was

going to ask Judy to get them, but I'm particular about them and figured I should do it myself."

"I don't know what that is, but yeah. Sure," I said with a sigh. "Anything else?"

"Just a trip to the bank," she said. "And a couple of other stops. Quick. It won't take much time. And I need to help you choose that frame. You probably want some drawing paper and fancy pens, right? We should go to the art store. The one you favor in Central Square."

I glanced at the time on my phone. "Will's going to kill me for keeping you out all day, isn't he?"

Shannon shook her head. "Unlikely," she replied. "We just won't tell him any of the details. What he doesn't know won't hurt him."

"Yeah, that's exactly why he'll kill me." I tossed some bills on the table and glanced at her. "Are we getting you another lunch? Perhaps afternoon tea?"

"Don't say things like that unless you're serious. I've been trying to get the girls to skip the pedicures in favor of high tea one of these days. They weren't having it. They like tequila too much. However, if you're up for a stop at The Reserve at The Langham Hotel, you'll never find yourself sitting on another milk crate."

"Heavens to Betsy," I muttered. "I'm not dressed for that. We'll have to save tea for another time."

She bit her lip, holding back a small smile. "How about a frappe for the road?"

I stood, laughing. "We'll take the long way to Charlestown, and swing by Kelly's Roast Beef in Revere. How about that?"

She made a noise that was frighteningly close to a cat's purr. "There will always be a real chair in my office for you," she said.

PATRICK

THIS WAS my kind of afternoon. My inbox was blissfully empty, my belly was full with the best burger I'd had in weeks, and I was double-fisting beer and bourbon before two o'clock. If only every workday was punctuated with a lunch like this one.

The only thing that could make this better would be the complete absence of my chatterbox brothers.

Sam, god love him, believed it was his fatherly duty to regale us with tales of his son's every gurgle and hiccup. The youngster was enjoying sweet potatoes and avocados these days, and—I was told—this ensured his future as a genius.

Matt was no better but instead of effusive details about infant sleep patterns, he was busy being an irritable son of a bitch. That gig was usually reserved for me, and I didn't like sharing it with him.

I was secretly hoping I could melt into this booth without gaining their notice. When Matt set his phone down and shifted toward me, I knew I had no such luck.

"How was that trip to Maine?" The lunch crowd was

clearing out but Matt still had to raise his voice for me to hear him across the booth. He flipped his phone over, gave it a quick grin, and then swirled the remaining inch of bourbon around his glass. "Hanukkah, right?"

"Right." I laced my hands around my beer, nodding slowly. "That fucking trip was…a fucking trip."

"Yeah, Tiel said Andy wasn't pleased," Sam added.

"Oh, yeah? That's what she told your wife?" I asked, crossing my arms over my chest. "Because that's more than she's told me."

Matt held up his hand. "Slow down. What the hell happened?"

"I'll start the clock on this therapy session," Sam murmured.

"First off, fuck you." I pointed at Sam. "Second, Andy didn't want to go. Her mother takes holidays extremely seriously, and Andy has no patience for being observant on occasion," I said. "But we went, smiling and nodding and keeping the comments about all of that to ourselves. Then, on the first night of Hanukkah, we're enjoying brisket and latkes and the whole bit, and Andy's stepfather says he and her mother have an announcement."

"I assume they weren't getting a puppy," Sam mused.

"Not a puppy." I shook my head. "They're getting a divorce."

"Oh, shit," Matt murmured.

"And that was a bombshell best dropped over dinner?" Sam asked. "Tiel's family is nuttier than a bag of trail mix, but that's pretty bold."

"Exactly. Thank you," I replied. "As if the announcement wasn't adequate, Andy's mom goes on to take down the entire institution of marriage. It's a construct of patriarchal oppression intended to control women."

"To be honest," Matt interrupted, "that was my thought process when getting married."

"I had the same thought," Sam added. "Turns out it doesn't work that way."

I spared them an irritated glare. "She said marriage is equivalent to indentured servitude. Humans aren't meant for monogamy—"

"So, we can assume she's the cheater," Sam quipped.

"I don't think so, but I don't know much of anything," I replied. "I kept refilling the wine glasses and listening while she repeatedly told my fiancée that she should never get married. That it was the biggest regret of her life, and she didn't want the same fate for her daughter."

"While the stepfather and current husband sat there?" Sam asked.

"Who do you think was drinking all the wine?" I asked.

"That's fantastic," Matt said, gesturing to the waiter for another round. "That is just fucking fantastic."

"Pretty much." I downed my beer. "We left the next morning and talked about the North End project she's working on with Riley the entire way home. We haven't discussed anything on the topic of weddings or marriage since then."

"I hate to be contrary," Matt started, "but I don't think you were discussing anything on the topic of weddings or marriage *before* last weekend. This might not be a valid data point."

"Yes, we were," I said, defensiveness thick in my words. "We were. We talked about it. Often."

"Yeah, I am not referring to the wedding cake versus mini pie versus doughnut argument," Matt replied. "I mean setting a date. Picking a venue. Making actual plans."

"We've done that," I said. Defensive as fuck.

"No, you haven't," Sam said, shaking his head.

"It's great how you two think you know everything," I said.

"That's because we do," Sam argued. "I don't know what you think the girls talk about when they get their nails done but it's not dust ruffles and casserole recipes."

I accepted a fresh tumbler of bourbon from the server and sank back against the booth as I sipped.

Realistically, Andy and I hadn't made many plans. At first, it didn't seem as though anything had changed. I'd asked, she'd accepted, the ring found a home on her finger. We were engaged and neither of us was in any rush to cross another threshold right away.

But that was more than a year ago.

We'd postponed all wedding talk until after the holidays last year, and that was fine. Closing out the year was always chaotic, and I required time to settle into the idea of being engaged to Andy.

We'd lazed in bed on New Year's Day, brainstorming dates. We'd debated seasons and argued about locations. Batted around ideas but committed to nothing. The cake-pie-doughnut controversy. Big wedding parties, tiny wedding parties. Restaurants we favored and hoped to hire for catering.

But the problem with large families like mine was that getting everyone in the same place on the same day—without resorting to rendition—required extreme flexibility. More flexibility than I possessed. I couldn't deal with the calculus of it all. I wanted a date, a time, a place, and I was prepared to wait as long as necessary.

Until I wasn't.

I realized I couldn't wait anymore around Abby's first birthday last month. It hit me then that I'd asked Andy to marry me almost one year prior, and we were no closer to making that a reality.

I couldn't wait anymore.

"I could be wrong," Sam said, snapping me out of my thoughts, "but Andy doesn't strike me as the type of woman who needs or wants to talk about everything. She deals with shit, and then she moves on."

"You're right about that," I conceded. "It's the 'moving on' that has me concerned. It seems like she's having second thoughts. I wouldn't be surprised if she wanted to call it all off, or not go forward with getting married."

"But she's also a processer," Matt added. "She thinks things through before she has thoughts or questions. She probably needs this time to sort it all out. If she wanted to pump the brakes, she'd have no problem telling you that."

I shrugged though they weren't wrong. "That's also true but"—I ran my hands through my hair—"I was going to book the honeymoon as her Christmas gift. I had it all planned out, and I was ready to pull the trigger."

I'd hoped to nail down a date after our trip to Maine. I had suggestions ready, and I'd confirmed the availability of several venues. I also had the city's best wedding planner queued up, and I was prepared to spend an exorbitant amount of money to make all of Andy's Pinterest dreams come true.

But then we sat through the dinner from hell, and I didn't know up from down anymore.

"You can't use the honeymoon as a Christmas gift," Sam argued. "It's the wedding gift, asshole."

"While Sam is correct," Matt said, stroking his chin, "I see the conflict you're now facing."

"Multiple conflicts." I glanced between them. "Not only is she questioning whether she wants to get married—"

"You're assuming that to be fact," Matt interrupted. "I seriously doubt your assumption."

"Let's go crazy and assume it is fact. Is that actually an issue?" Sam asked. "I mean, yes, it blows, but it's not like she's leaving you."

"Yeah, she and Riley are going to be working on that North End project for time immemorial," Matt added. "She's not going anywhere."

"Right," Sam replied, clinking his glass against Matt's. "Here's the real question, Optimus. Do you need to be married to be happy?"

I started to respond but then stopped myself. I wanted Andy. I wanted to be married to her, but if that wasn't an option for me, I'd survive with whichever alternatives she offered. I'd take whatever she was willing to give and I'd be content with it.

But for all that contentment, I also knew I wanted her to be my wife and I didn't want any of this noise to get in our way.

"It's complicated," I said eventually.

"No shit," Matt said, laughing. "It wouldn't be group therapy if it wasn't complicated."

"And now I need a less controversial gift," I said.

"Yeah, let's get serious about this excursion." Matt pushed aside his plate and pulled a pen and piece of folded paper from his pocket. "I've put together a list of shops."

"Shocking. Jugger has a spreadsheet," Sam said under his breath.

"We can go big and start with jewelry," Matt continued, tapping his pen against the paper. "Or brave the crowds at Copley Plaza where we have a variety of retail options. Clothes, handbags, that shop with the bath bombs, more jewelry."

I hated malls almost as much as I hated faux wood paneling.

"I'd rather contract leprosy than go to Copley," I said.

Matt clicked his pen and drew a line through one of the entries on his list. "I have bookstores, the pedicure place, assorted gift shops, lingerie boutiques, the place with the funky wooden bowls, everything." He glanced up. "Do any of those sound good, or is everything on par with leprosy?"

"It's all leprosy," I said. "Can't I just hire someone to bring me a range of gifts and I choose the ones I like best?"

"You can," Matt said at length. "I don't know if that's a good idea, but I'm beginning to doubt whether any of this is a good idea."

He rubbed his eyes. He looked fucking exhausted.

"What's wrong with you?" I asked, pointing at him.

"Nothing." He shook his head and returned to his list. "I'm just tired. I haven't been sleeping this week."

"Please don't tell us about your sex life," Sam said. "Those details are best left unsaid."

"It's funny how you managed to grow some decency," I said to him. "Or do you turn back into a manwhore at sundown?"

Sam wiggled his ring finger. "No, it's permanent."

Matt pressed his palms to his eyes. "Can we get back on topic?"

I lifted my bourbon, pointing it toward Matt. "Be my guest."

He shook his head and glanced down at his list. "If you want a personal shopper's assistance, Patrick, you should call Shannon. I'm sure she has one in her address book."

"Don't do that," Sam said. "You'd fire this person within twenty minutes and that's not the way to start a holiday vacation."

"Then I'm out of solutions," I said.

"I have plenty of solutions right here," Matt said, waving his list at me. "Quit the bitching and decide where you want to start."

"I have no fucking clue," I murmured. "Lingerie, I guess. I don't know."

"It would be weird for us to buy lingerie together," Sam said. "Right? Wouldn't it be weird?"

"I believe the question is whether we *should* buy lingerie together," I said.

"What is the big deal?" Matt asked. He shook his head, impatient with our refusal to jump at the idea of communal underwear shopping. Because it was so fucking normal.

"It's not a big deal. I just don't need moral support to pick out fancy underwear, and I don't like the idea of either of you seeing anything I'd choose for Andy."

"I have no intention of looking at anything you purchase," Matt argued. "We can go in separately if that puts your twisted mind at ease."

"We have to compare because we don't want to get the same thing. They'd know. They talk about this shit. Hell," I said, pointing to Sam, "your wife knows more about Andy's feelings about our disastrous trip to Maine than I do because these women tell each other every fucking thing."

Matt scrubbed his hands down his face as he yawned. "Then we'll ask the saleslady to make sure we buy different things."

"What happens then? You're in the office with Andy two months from now and you're wondering if she's wearing the panties I got her for Christmas. I'd have to kill you, and I really don't have time to find a place to hide your body."

"You're overthinking this," Matt said, "and I'm worried about your sanity. I'm truly concerned."

"I can assure you that the only underwear I think about is that belonging to my wife," Sam said. "Until you mentioned it just now, I was oblivious to the notion that Andy and under-wear existed in the same universe."

"That's probably a slight exaggeration, don't you think?" Matt stared at Sam.

"No," Sam replied. "Not at all."

"Leprosy," I said. "Give me the leprosy."

"Let's not forget that lingerie is a highly selfish gift." Sam reached across the table and snatched Matt's list. "I'm going to enjoy it more than Tiel."

"Disagree," Matt said, grabbing the paper back from Sam. "A good gift is something she won't buy for herself. Lauren only allows herself to buy new things every few months and she always waits for the sales. She'll love it, and that's why her favorite shop, Forty Winks, is on here."

"That last place on your list is interesting," Sam said, a smug grin on his face. "Care to share some news with everyone?"

"Shut up," Matt snapped. "I mean it. Shut the fuck up. Not a word."

I didn't know what they were arguing about and I didn't care. "Both of you should shut up," I grumbled. "Let's start with the lacy shit and then move onto jewelry. If those don't work, bookstores and gift shops."

"Sounds like a plan," Matt said, jotting some notes. "Burgers, beer, bourbon…and bras."

"And for fuck's sake, let's find some pubs to visit along the way," I said. The waiter dropped our tab on the table and I took a moment to glare at the total. "There's no reason to shop sober."

"Okay, then," Sam murmured. "I guess I'll drive."

I pushed the tab toward him. "You're paying, too."

I GLANCED up at the brownstone's front window but dropped my gaze when I noticed the corseted mannequin. I didn't know the rules for this. I'd never shopped for unmentionables before and I wasn't convinced I was up to the task.

"Well?" Matt gestured to the short stone staircase leading to the shop's door. "Are we going in or would you boys rather stay out here and freeze your dicks off on the sidewalk all afternoon?"

"I'm going in." Sam moved past us and climbed the stairs. "And let's try to be as normal as possible today."

Matt clapped me on the back, nodding. "He's talking to you."

"I can't see why," I replied as I trailed them up the steps.

"Because you're scowling and you look like you want to rip the doors off the hinges," Sam said.

"And I wouldn't be surprised if you asked a saleswoman her cup size," Matt added.

"I would *never* do that," I hissed as we stepped inside.

"I'm not getting involved in that debate," Sam murmured. He held up his hands, demanding our attention. "Here's the plan. We're going to divide and conquer without crossing swords. No need to talk or make eye contact."

"I had no idea that you're both raving lunatics," Matt murmured. "Or whichever brand of psychosis this is."

Sam ignored him and barreled on. "Patrick, you're staying

in the front section with the robes and scarves. You're going to ease in, and work your way up to the good stuff."

"I'm not even close to drunk enough for this," I said.

This time, Sam ignored me as he continued with his game plan. "Matt is going to start over there, at that table with all the panties."

"I was really hoping to die before hearing either of you utter the word *panties*," I said. "I'm running out of goals over here, guys."

"Panties," Sam repeated. "While you two go to your corners, I'm going to the back wall to look at—at—at—my wife picking out a black leather corset."

I followed Sam's gaze, but it wasn't the woman wearing the bright blue dress with tiny silver stars who caught my attention. It was the mass of dark, curly hair beside her. "My fiancée seems to favor the red satin variety."

"Do you think the dressing rooms are reasonably private?" Sam asked. "I don't need a soundproof room or anything. Just a closed door."

I pointed at the ceiling in a vague gesture toward the late eighties Sade song pounding from the speakers. "Yes."

"We've made it weird." Matt stepped between us. "I'm going to look at those panties now," he said, "and only the panties. I'm gonna keep my head down and I'm probably gonna look like a perv since I'll be fondling underwear with single-minded focus but I don't want to see anything else until we're done. Someone holler when it's time to leave."

I WENT after Andy without a single idea of what I'd say or do once I had her attention. And I didn't care who was watching. I followed her around the corner and down a shadowy corridor lined with large oil paintings. They were filthy, but in the most tastefully depraved way.

She knew I was a few steps behind. The grin she tossed over her shoulder was proof of it. That, and she didn't close the door when she stepped into the last dressing room.

"Hello there," she said when I closed the door. I kept my hand pressed there. I wasn't sure whether I was holding it shut or holding myself steady. "We don't meet like this often enough."

Drawing a breath to cool the tension pumping through my body, I pushed away from the door and leaned back against the wall. "I thought you were shopping for kitchenware."

Andy turned her attention to arranging her items on the rack, shuffling the bras, panties, and other lacy bits that defied naming conventions. The red corset that started all of this. She selected a nothing of lace that would meet with certain death under my hands and studied it carefully. "I can use this in the kitchen," she said.

Her gaze was easy, as if we were standing in the middle of a paint store and comparing shades of gray rather than a velvet-draped sin emporium.

She looked up at me then—*finally*—and the smile tugging at her lips was nothing short of devious. I lunged for her, batting the lacy fire starter out of her grip and seizing her hips. "If you think you're wearing that in the kitchen, you're not going to get much cooking done."

Her fingers scraped up my neck and into my hair, forcing a shiver from her touch. She knew how to bring me to heel, and I loved it. It wasn't even funny how much this woman owned me. How much I wanted her to own me.

I want to be married to you.

I poured those words into fast, frantic kisses, but it wasn't enough. With my hands on her tight little ass, I boosted her up and flattened her against the wall. Hangers clattered to the floor and I heard the chandelier rattling above us, but none of that stopped me from grinding into her.

"Unzip me," I ordered between kisses. "Take my cock out."

As Andy palmed my length, a knock sounded at the door. "Hello in there! It's Heather. What can I do for you? How is everything fitting? Is there anything I can grab for you? Different sizes or colors?"

"Not a word out of you," Andy whispered. She slapped a hand over my lips as I started to respond. "I'm all set for now, Heather."

"Okay," she said slowly. "I thought I heard you call for me but I'll just leave you to it."

That earned me a pointed glare. I shrugged. I couldn't help it.

"Thanks, Heather," she replied.

Andy stared at the door, her hand still covering my mouth and my erection throbbing for her attention, and listened while Heather knocked on several other doors. Once her voice faded away, I rocked between Andy's legs again and squeezed her ass.

"Someone's feeling bold today," she murmured.

"You're teasing me with talk of cooking in four inches of lace," I replied. "Not sure how you expected me to respond to that."

"I'd planned on teasing you with it on Christmas morning, but you can't beg, stalk, and choose."

"I'm certain that I can," I said, nipping at her neck.

She planted a chaste kiss on my jaw and tipped her head to the side. "Since you're here, you can sit right over there"—I followed her gaze to the velvet slipper chair in the corner —"and see the pieces I'm considering."

I thrust against her again and drew a breathy moan from her lips. "I'd rather see them from right here."

Her gaze cooled and she aimed that same steel-spined, take-neither-prisoners-nor-shit look that she reserved for errant contractors at me. "You can sit over there or you can leave."

With a frustrated growl, I set her on her feet. "I'm not leaving, Kitten."

I retreated to the corner while Andy collected the pieces I'd knocked over in my haste to get my hands on her. Once everything was in her preferred order, she stripped out of her clothes. And it was every bit *stripping*.

When she turned away from me and wiggled out of her jeans, exposing her skimpy black panties, I had to press my knuckles to my mouth to repress a growl. Even after nearly five years, Andy still leveled me.

"How did this happen? Did you…did you follow me here?" she asked, ripping me out of my unabashed appreciation for her body. I folded my hands over my fly in a weak attempt to conceal my erection. I wasn't sure why I bothered.

"I did not," I replied, staring at her bare skin. She was nude save for undies and menorah knee socks, and I was a breath away from drooling. "This was all Matt's idea."

She considered this for a moment and then nodded as if she could understand his logic. "He knows what Lauren likes."

I dragged my gaze from her eyes to her feet. "I didn't think this was your style," I said, jerking my chin toward the items hanging on the rack.

She crossed her arms under her bare breasts and arched an eyebrow. She went right on staring at me, cool and calm while

I was about to tear this tiny room apart. "I'm going to try these on now." She pointed at the door. "Last chance to leave."

I lifted my hands and gestured toward the tent in my trousers. "I'm long past that, Kitten."

She reached for a frilly bra in a shade of beige that looked boring on walls and fucking delicious as it met her skin. "You didn't have to come in here," she said, her voice filled with playful censure. She stared at herself in the mirror, shifting to get a look at the bra's ornate back.

"Oh, yes, I did." I stared as she adjusted her breasts in the cups, palming and lifting them until they were seated just right. "There was no way in hell I was letting you check out these things without some supervision."

I leaned forward and sucked her nipple through the fabric. She dropped her hands to my shoulders, her nails driving into my sweater as I tugged her skin between my teeth.

"Is that what you're doing? Supervising?" she said through a moan.

"Yes. Get this one," I murmured, kissing my way down to her belly button. "Next."

I watched while she cycled through several more bras, each more arresting than the one before, and knew I was bound to leave bites on my knuckles and zipper marks on my cock today. Andy didn't even have to work at teasing me. I couldn't get enough of her, alternately stamping my approval on each piece with kisses and bites and flattening her against the wall while I devoured her lips.

I jerked my chin toward the items hanging from satin hangers as she unhooked one particularly heart-stopping bra. "Any favorites?" I asked.

She smiled at the sexy scraps, and then back at me. "I have a few ideas but I'm curious which are your favorites. You seem to have some strong"—her gaze dropped between my legs —"opinions."

I shook my head as I watched her pull on a sheer black kimono-robe-thing. I almost swallowed my tongue. "None of them," I said, my voice like gravel. "The lace does nothing for me."

Andy waved at the plush room and the desire pulsing in the air around us, a smug smile on her lips. "Are you sure about that?"

"Quite," I answered.

That earned me a sharp "Hm" and an arched eyebrow. She turned away from me while she held up two bras by the hangers, and I stole that moment to capture the kimono's fabric between my thumb and forefinger. It was soft and silky, not unlike her long hair.

"It's not the lace," I said. "It's the skin."

Andy turned, her gaze warm. It was hard to pay compliments to her as she didn't find most of them authentic, but every time I struck the right spot, it made the slight pinking of her cheeks all the more special.

"You're just saying that," she whispered, her hands on her hips.

I hooked my finger around the ribbon keeping the kimono shut and gave it a yank. She stumbled forward, and I steered her into my lap. "If you don't believe me, let me prove it." I held her with one hand splayed across her ass while I fought my belt and zipper. "You torture me," I said, edging her panties to the side.

I should've taken time to warm her up, get her ready. I knew what she needed but I didn't want to give today. But now, with my cock drowning in the heat at her entrance, I wanted to take. I wanted to punish her.

For teasing me.

For making me wait.

For making me wonder.

I slammed into her and pressed my fingers deep into her skin. A primal roar gathered in my chest, one that didn't feel altogether human. I kept my lips on her neck—there would be a mark there tomorrow—and hands on her hips, moving her as I wanted. If the only thing I could claim was her body, I was taking it.

Her fingers were in my hair, twisting and pulling with every brutal thrust. The chandelier was rattling, the walls shaking, the chair under my ass shaking. Heather was probably listening to every moan, but I didn't care if the entire city listened to me fucking my fiancée.

"Andy, I want—"

The words were there. Right fucking there. And like a weight carried long past the point of exhaustion, I was ready to set them down and never see them again.

"Andy," I started, "I want—"

"Hush," she said, pressing her fingertips to my lips. My gaze traveled down at her fingers until landing on the platinum ring, the one with the diamond lazing toward her pinky finger. She'd called it ostentatious. She'd called it excessive. She'd called it an outdated tradition. But then, after her long list of reasons why it wasn't right and all of my rebuttals, she'd called it perfect. And all of that? It was perfect, for us.

Looking into her eyes, I hammered into her without mercy. I was being rough and she'd be sore later, but I'd kiss it better. With her parted legs in mind, I growled and dropped my head to her shoulder.

"I know what you want. Just take it," Andy whispered. "Take *me*."

My brain heard those words and *boom*. My orgasm went from gathering at the base of my spine to barreling through my body like a runaway train. I shouted her name as I surged inside her, surrendering to some primitive need to fuck her like I meant it.

My cock pulsed for hours, or so it seemed. When I was capable of breathing, thinking, and opening my eyes at once, I peppered Andy's neck and shoulders with light kisses.

Right now, with my hands on her skin and my cock half hard inside her, I regretted everything. Taking, punishing, thinking any of that would ease the tension inside me.

"You didn't," I said.

She shook her head. "No, but that doesn't mean it was bad," she said. "And I know you're good for it."

I ran my hands along her back, savoring her small shiver at my touch. "Tonight," I vowed. I wanted to touch her and taste her, and beg her for all the things I craved. "I'll make it up to you."

"There are no checks and balances when it comes to orgasms. We both had a good time. That's all that matters."

"It matters to me," I said. There were enough problems in my world. I didn't have to add *inconsiderate lover* to the list.

She pressed her lips to mine. I could feel her smile. "Matt and Sam are probably waiting for you," she said.

"I don't fucking care," I replied, and that was the damn truth. I wasn't concerned with the universe beyond the walls of this room.

"You should go," she said, untangling herself from my lap. "I have to finish my shopping, and I imagine you do, too."

"Doesn't mean I want to," I grumbled. I stood, tucking my dick away with great reluctance. I watched as Andy pulled on her clothes and shook out her hair, and then rearranged the hangers. "Get all of them." I moved toward the door but stopped to study the kimono. It was nothing more than shapeless fabric on the hanger but the thought of her nipples pebbled against that sheer black had my cock pulsing with need. "Definitely this one. I want you in this tonight."

Andy flattened her hand between my shoulder blades and pushed me into the hall. "Go," she ordered. "I'll see you at home."

"But the kimono—"

"Go," she repeated, laughing.

I took a step toward the sales floor but then turned back to Andy. Striding toward her, I drove my hands into her hair and brought my lips hers. "Not yet," I said, dragging her lower lip between my teeth. I kissed her again, my eyes fixed on hers, and stroked my thumbs over her delicate cheeks. "Buy that kimono. Finish your shopping. Get your ass home."

Andy nodded, and I stepped back into the hall. There, I found myself watching while Tiel dismissed Sam from a dressing room two doors down.

"You heard nothing, saw nothing," I said. "I'll swear to the same."

Sam stared at the plush rug under his feet, his hands on his hips as he shook his head. "Deal," he said. "Let's go."

"What?" Sam snapped when we found Matt on the sidewalk. He was carrying a large gift bag and wagging his finger at us with more glee than a grown man should be able to muster.

"Look at that sloppy grin on Optimus's face," he replied, pointing at me. "And look at you, Stark. You're saltier than soy sauce."

"Your point being?" I asked with an impatient sigh. My

dick was still wet and my head was fuzzy, and I had little patience for my brother's ribbing.

"My point," Matt started, gesturing between us again, "is that I would've expected it to be the other way around."

I glanced at Sam, looking for some explanation of this bullshit. He shrugged, then pulled his phone from his back pocket. He tapped at the screen, seemingly writing a short novel, before saying, "I have no idea what you're talking about."

"The dressing rooms," Matt said at length.

"What's the next stop on that list of yours?" Sam asked. "Obviously, I struck out here."

"The pub," I barked. "The only place we're going now is the pub."

"Fuck, yes," Sam murmured. "I need a fucking drink."

"Really thought it would be the other way around," Matt said under his breath.

"Maybe you should stop," I said. "The fact you're thinking about it at all is unnecessary."

"We should've dragged Riley along," Sam said. "He would've knocked over a table or asked for a demonstration on the proper way to lace a corset."

"That's true," I said.

"All right," Matt said. "We'll bring him next time."

"We're never doing this again," Sam said. He turned to me. "Right?"

I shrugged. "I could be persuaded."

Matt pressed his fist to his mouth as he laughed. "Really thought it was going to be the other way around."

"Shut the hell up," I said. "Can we go to the pub now?"

Sam: In case I die this afternoon, I want you to know one
thing.
Sam: You're wicked.
Sam: Wicked wicked wicked.
Sam: You could drop a house on someone and that wouldn't
be as wicked as the stunt you pulled today.
Sam: I hope you're happy.
Sam: I'm going to drink this erection away now, but when I get
home, your mouth will be spending some time with my cock.

WHEN I MADE it home that evening, after stopping at
several taverns, making a jewelry store pilgrimage, and
depositing Matt and Patrick in their neighborhoods, I was
suffering from the most virulent case of blue balls in my entire
existence. I wanted nothing more than to take Tiel by the hand,
and get her behind closed doors and on her knees.

After instituting *and* enforcing a strict look-but-don't-touch rule in the dressing room, she deserved it. Then, after working off the worst of this afternoon's aggression, I wanted to get her into that leather corset and fuck her like I adored her. I did, and she deserved that, too.

But I found Tiel deep in conversation with Ellie, who—while carrying on a conversation—was also making a valiant effort at teaching my son the basics of drumming. With a stock pot and wooden spoon.

We didn't get enough time with Ellie. Her band's touring schedule was grueling, and these visits were few and far between. She'd originally planned to spend the holidays in England with her girlfriend, but things soured between them recently. I didn't know all the details but it was obvious Ellie was licking some wounds.

I watched them talk for several minutes, still concealed in the darkened doorway, and couldn't help smiling to myself. Dave was making a holy racket but looked happier than when he had a spoonful of peanut butter all to himself. And my wife—there was never a time when I didn't enjoy staring at her.

I was especially fond of staring at her while she debated which bras and corsets would do the most good for her cleavage. The short answer to that question was all of them.

"I don't believe that," Ellie said, shock rippling through her voice. "Not you. Never you. Tell me this is a myth."

That pulled me right out of my fantasies and away from the door.

Tiel shrugged as she ran her hands over Dave's teddy bear. "We can't really take an infant with us."

"Maybe not all the time, no," Ellie replied. "But you hire babysitters. You bargain with one of your seventeen in-laws. You get some noise-canceling headphones for the kiddo. You call in the cool aunt to help you. You don't pick out a pair of mom jeans, get your hair frosted, and pack your life before children away in the attic."

"What are we talking about?" I sat down on the mat with them and held out my hands to Dave. He replied with a drooly squeal and excitedly beat his hands on the pot.

"Nothing," Tiel murmured, shaking her head.

"It's not nothing," Ellie hissed. "She said you two haven't been out since Dave was born."

"That's not what I said." Tiel shot a pointed look at Ellie. "Don't start, El."

"We go out all the time," I argued. "Sunday dinners at Matt and Lauren's loft. Our summer trip to Cape Cod. All those roof deck parties at Patrick and Andy's place. We visit with Shannon and Will, and their daughter, all the time."

"Yeah, prepster," Ellie replied. "You have lots of outings *with* your child. That's not wrong. You are stellar parents. I'm not disputing any of that. I'm just saying you can't forget who were before Dave was born."

"We haven't really wanted to go anywhere without him," Tiel argued. "Riley will watch him for a bit so we can sleep in or catch up on work. He'll take him to the park or out for a walk, and I can get in some practice time. Or a shower. That's all we need right now."

I glanced at my wife, hoping her expression would explain the note of surrender in her voice, but she was focused on the teddy bear. Her thumbs passed over its ears and down its face, over and over, and in this moment, I wasn't certain I knew anything at all.

"I've been here all week and I haven't seen Riley once," Ellie said. "When is all of this happening? Why can't he give you a night out"—she waved her hands at me and Tiel —"*together*?"

"He's seeing someone," Tiel said. "He spends most of his time at her place now. It's kind of serious."

When I walked through the door, I believed my wife was sexy and confident, and steeped in the satisfaction of having everything she could ever want. This was the woman who'd teased me within an inch of my life earlier today.

But as she stroked the bear's dark blue ears, I realized she was missing something. *We* were missing something.

We'd spent every minute of the months since Dave's birth —and many of the minutes before it, too—putting all of our collective energy into giving him the best of everything. We didn't have to announce that we were actively attempting to right the wrongs of our own childhoods, though there were countless moments when I picked up my son and spoke to him with love because I knew my father never did that to me.

And still, we were missing something. We were missing each other. It was possible that we found each other this afternoon, and we needed to hold onto that.

Ellie's gaze pinged between us as she shook her head. "I cannot believe what I'm hearing." She crouched down to Dave's eye level. "All right, little buddy. Here's what we're going to do. Auntie El is sending your mom and dad on a date," she said. "Can you believe they've been married for almost two years already? It was the most badass surprise and an epic party, and they need to have that kind of fun. D'you think they can manage that?"

Dave let out a deep belly laugh as he thumped a spoon against the pot. I glanced at Tiel again, and found her staring at me. I shrugged, and she replied with a quick shrug of her own.

"None of that," Ellie said, wagging a spoon at us. "You're going." She pointed the spoon at the staircase. "Go change into something cute. Going-out cute, not 'I teach third graders how to hold a violin' cute. Then you can tell me the seven thousand things you want to tell me about caring for your kid."

———

"WHERE...WHERE SHOULD WE GO?" Tiel asked once we were settled into the car. "Every spot that comes to mind is relatively quiet and child-friendly, and I can't think of anywhere in the city that doesn't fit into those categories."

It took her no time at all to change into a cute dress that was technically conservative—high neck, long sleeves, knee-length skirt—but destroyed me every time she wore it. While I drooled all over her, she snuggled Dave, gave Ellie some quick pointers, and jotted down my siblings' phone numbers. My brain was stalled on that dress, and hadn't caught up with this conversation.

"Anywhere you want, Sunshine," I replied, still eyeing her curves.

"Yeah—but—that's—I mean," she stammered. "I don't know."

"Let me make this easy for you," I said. "Deuxave, L'Espalier, or Bondir. Your choice."

She shook her head. "No, Sam, no. That's ridiculous. We don't need the posh restaurant scene when we can just as easily get tacos."

"Not an option, " I said, leveling a stern gaze at her. "You need a night out and I need to spoil you. When was the last time you had a dirty martini? Or five?"

She gestured toward her breasts. I had no problem dragging my eyes there. "I'll have to pump and dump when we get home."

"That's okay," I said gently. "You have enough pumped milk in the fridge and freezer to give him a few bottles."

She bit her lip and glanced back at the house. Dave was born small, and the doctors wanted to see him gain weight quickly. That meant feeding him twice as much as the average infant, and pumping between nursing sessions. He was fat and happy now, all chubby cheeks and baby rolls, but I knew Tiel carried a lot of anxiety about keeping him in fighting shape. She guarded that freezer stash like a state secret.

"I'm taking you to Deuxave. If you hate it, you can spend the night tormenting me like you did earlier today," I said. "That will make it really easy for me to divest you of your clothes, shred your panties, and fuck you like I paid for it."

"Are you still upset about this afternoon?" she asked.

"Upset?" I repeated. I grabbed her hand and pressed it to my zipper. "Does this feel *upset* to you?"

One side of her mouth tipped up in a smile, but she didn't respond.

"Tell me what you're thinking," I ordered, rubbing the back of her hand as she stroked me. "What's going on in there?"

"Do you want to do this? We don't have to. Really. I know you've had a busy week and—"

"Yes, I definitely want to do this," I said, cutting her off. I released my hold on her wrist. She liked it when I forced her, just a bit, but she wasn't liking it now. "There's never a time when I don't want you all to myself. You have no idea how much I need my Tiel time."

"I need Sam time," she said.

"Then let's go," I said. "We'll see where the night takes us."

We ended up having a simple, civilized dinner outing. We ate, we drank, we talked about our son. There was no suggestion of destroying panties or my dick in her mouth. She knew what I wanted. She was going to come to me when she was ready for it.

"Why don't we go over to Sligo's?" I slipped my credit card back into my wallet and glanced across the table at Tiel. "Or the Middle East. I'm sure there's something interesting going on there."

She narrowed her eyes. "Why would you want to do that? They don't even dice the cucumbers for you at Sligo's."

"Why not?" I asked. "We're out. We have a reliable babysitter. Neither of us have to work tomorrow. Cucumbers aside, why shouldn't we?"

It looked as though Tiel intended to refute my claims, but then she pursed her lips, nodded to herself, and said, "Let's do it."

We stopped at a number of our old haunts, venues we hadn't visited since before Dave was born, but this wasn't a great night for live music. Either it was the fiercely cold weather or the proximity to the holidays keeping folks away, or we just didn't know the best spots anymore. Eventually, we ended up at the bar we'd visited after that scorching day spent in a stalled elevator.

"A lot has changed since I came here the first time," I said over the rim of my drink, "with you."

"I haven't thought about that night in ages but I remember it like it was yesterday," Tiel said, awe ringing in her words. "It was so bizarre. Everything about it, totally bizarre."

"I wanted you that night," I confessed.

"You wanted to fuck me," she said, lifting her glass to her lips. "Big difference."

"Yeah, I wanted to fuck you," I said, laughing.

"You wanted to fuck everyone." She took a sip of her drink, her eyebrow arched in challenge just as it had been years ago.

"Not after that night," I said. "Not once." Tiel glanced away, a slight grin tugging at her lips. I liked that. I wanted her to have all the victories and possessiveness in the world. I wanted her to feel like she'd won something special with me because that was how I felt about her. "I want you tonight, too."

"Yeah," she murmured, her body swaying with the pulsing music. "You mentioned something about that earlier."

I plucked her drink from her fingertips and set it down. Then I leaned into her, pressing her back against the bar and dragging my knuckles along the line of her neck. "I spent the afternoon counting down the minutes until I could get you alone again," I whispered against her skin. "I'd been hoping Ellie would want some time with the baby tonight because, after that stunt in the lingerie shop, I've been dying to get my hands on you."

"What stunt?" she asked, her brows quirking up as she reached under my suit coat and settled her hands on my waist. "I don't remember any stunts."

"No?" I asked as my lips met the tender skin near her ear. "How would you describe this afternoon's events?"

"I believe we bumped into each other while running errands," she said, a pulse of faux-indignation heavy in her words. "You invited yourself over, selected some unmentionables for me, and requested that I try them on. Then, you articulated the ways you'd ruin each item. It was exceptionally rude."

"So rude," I agreed, taking her earlobe between my teeth. "But you were looking at naughty lingerie, my wife, and you wouldn't let me touch you. Can you blame me?"

She shook her head and ran her hands up my back. "I've never blamed you for being rude," she said. "But I will have a problem if you don't help me find a storage room or broom closet right now."

"MAYBE WE SHOULD JUST GO HOME," Tiel said.

She was gnawing on her bottom lip and staring at the road ahead with doubtful eyes.

"We're not going home," I snapped. "We're finding somewhere semi-private to get you naked and on my cock, and that's the end of it."

"But we can do that at home," she argued. "That would save us time, actually. It doesn't make sense to keep popping into different bars at the off chance they'll have a dark corner available."

"I've never known you to choose the path of convention," I replied.

"It's like we're on sex pub crawl," she said. From the sound of it, she wasn't nearly as enthusiastic about this adventure as she was two hours ago. Admittedly, I was tired and frustrated but I was committed. "A wild sex goose chase. And for what? To remind ourselves we still know how to have a good time?" She turned, giving me an *oh please* glare. "I can have a good time. Don't you doubt that. Just because I'm a mom now doesn't mean I'm not fun. I am *tons* of fun."

I drummed my fingers against the steering wheel. It was all I could do because laughing was the wrong reaction. I knew that much.

"Just pull over," she ordered, gesturing to the side of the road. We were in the middle of Cambridge, and as if street parking wasn't a big enough issue here, the sidewalks were packed with people heading home from bars and clubs. "We'll do it here. In the car."

"We'll do *what* in the car?"

"Sex," she replied as if it was completely obvious. "We'll have sex. Right here. This is fine. Just pull over."

"Yeah, that's not going to happen." I shook my head. "You're fun, you're sexy, you're fucking amazing. You're a wicked tease, too. Being those things doesn't require you to also get arrested for public indecency or lewd and lascivious behavior."

"But I love it when you're lewd," she purred. "Lascivious, too."

I came to a stop at a red light and glanced at my wife. Her smile was wide and bright, her eyes shining with excitement. "This rebellious streak of yours," I mused, tucking her hair over her ear.

She edged her skirt up, teasing it higher on her thighs. "What about it?"

A montage of options passed through my mind until I felt her rebelliousness pulling me under, wrapping around me, throwing off the bow lines of comfort and civility.

"You're sure about this?" I dropped my hand onto her stocking-clad thigh. "About me taking you in the car? Where anyone could walk by and see you begging for it?"

The light turned green.

"I'm sure."

With a single nod, I drove through the intersection. It only required a few turns to leave the glare of street lights and the roar of nightlife crowds behind. In that time, my hand made its way up her thigh and between her legs. She pretended she was unaffected by my touch but the subtle rock of her hips said otherwise.

I drove down a dark lane and into the last driveway. Tiel tilted her head to get a look at the house. "What are we doing?" she asked. "Where are we?"

"The Federal restoration," I said simply. "The one I started working on last month." I clicked the headlights off. "Quiet neighborhood, vacant property. Still suitably public to meet your demands for fun and lewd, but I don't have to worry about drunk kids from MIT watching you ride my cock. I have my kinks, Sunshine, but that isn't one of them."

She leaned back, eyeing me up and down. "I got pretty lucky with you."

"Trust me. I'm the lucky one here." I tipped my chin toward the back seat. "Shall we?"

Tiel unbuckled her seat belt and threw off her scarf. "Meet you there."

We scrambled into the back, shucking coats and kicking off shoes as we went. We lunged for each other when we landed on the bench. It was uncoordinated, messy, nearly violent. I yanked her dress up while she whipped my belt from the loops, and then we worked together to get my trousers down just enough to access the essentials. It was too damn cold for full nudity, and we didn't have time for that either.

"Hurry, hurry, hurry," she whispered, straddling my lap.

I tapped the back of her legs, silently ordering her to rise up on her knees, and pinched the fine fabric of her stockings. I pulled until it gave way, a shrill sound echoing between us as it ripped. She sucked in a breath while I shredded the crotch.

"I was going to take them off," she said, completely straight-faced. "These are cool tights. Expensive, too. That was unnecessary, Sam."

With my palm between her legs, I rocked the heel against her mound. I grinned at the shuddering gasp she released, and the way she leaned into my touch. "I'll buy you many replacement pairs," I said, curling my fingers around the last scrap of fabric between me and her pussy. "Panties, too."

"What? Don't tear my—"

"What did you say, Sunshine? I didn't catch that." Just like that, all barriers were gone and my fingers were inside her. "I've been itching to do that all damn day."

She stared straight into my eyes. "You are such a beast," she whispered. "I still don't know why I like it."

"Not everything requires psychoanalysis." I slipped my fingers over her clit, painting it with her arousal, and nodded between us. "Get on my cock."

She took my shaft in hand, stroking with more patience and tenderness than I thought I could manage after two hours on the edge. *No.* No, I couldn't bear this. I needed rough and fast, like everything I'd imagined since walking out of that dressing room.

As she dragged me over her folds and my hands shifted to squeeze her ass, my head lolled back, torn between bliss and agony.

"Don't tease me, Tiel," I growled.

"Not teasing," she whispered, sinking down slowly. She hummed as she took me all the way to the root. I dug my fingers into her ass and forced her closer as she rocked against me like a dream. "Savoring the moment."

I thought I'd be able to do this. That I could let her set the pace, take what she needed. I couldn't. I thrust hard, forcing a startled cry from her lips. "Savor this, Sunshine."

There were going to be fingertip bruises on her backside tomorrow, of that I was certain. I was clinging to her, carving tiny notches into that supple flesh as I surged up into her body, hunting for any shred of her that I hadn't yet claimed. I pumped into her hard, harder when her lips landed on my neck and her teeth nipped at my skin.

This kind of sex didn't require conservation. It was going to be quick and rough. And awkward, with limbs and joints in all the wrong places. But it was going to shake the fucking earth. It was the kind of transcendental sex that I remembered vividly if not for its technique then for its meaning. This night and the day-long tease meant something, even if I didn't know what that was right now. And it didn't need running commentary on the incredible heat and wet of her pussy, or the relative hardness of my dick, or the furious need we had for each other. All of that was subtext.

It was enough to feel this, every second of it, because we needed that most of all.

"I can't hold out much longer," I said through a groan. "I need you there."

She nodded, anchoring her hands on my shoulders as she rocked into my thrusts. This angle was good—I was deep deep deep—but I couldn't stroke her clit without wedging a hand between us and twisting my arm to hit the right spot. I couldn't do anything but sit here, watching her find her release on her own.

It was torture. It was also hot as hell.

"Do you know how much I love watching you?" I asked, thrusting into her hard enough to see stars. She worked for it, and I couldn't think of anything more arousing than watching my wife use me like this. "Do you know? Do you have any idea what you do to me?"

"I—I—I," she gasped, her eyes closing, her lips parting, and her body quivering under my hands. "I'm going to—ah —going to—"

"That's right, baby," I whispered, my hands fused to her backside. "Come for me."

Her body spasmed, destroying the thin hold I had on my orgasm. It pumped out of me quickly, one huge pulse after another. She curled into my chest, her head on my shoulder. We were still panting from the exertion.

"Holy hell, Tiel, anytime you want to be a fun mom, I'm fucking here for it," I said with a sigh. "I can't believe I'm saying this, but I wouldn't mind visiting that lingerie shop again. I'd like to establish the ground rules before subjecting my cock to that kind of sweet agony but we can work those details out later. I don't think I can feel my legs right now. That was—"

"Oh, no," she said, sitting up abruptly. "Oh, no, please no."

"What's wrong?"

She dragged her bottom lip between her teeth and cringed. "I just let down."

She untangled her arms, and yeah, two large wet spots now dotted her dress. "Well," I started, brushing her hair back from her face, "now you don't have to pump when we get home." She laughed at that and I held my arms open to her. "Let me hold you for a minute. I'm not ready for this to be over yet."

"I'm going to get breast milk all over you," she said.

"I do not care." I beckoned her closer. "I want you right here, right now."

She returned to her spot on my chest and I let my eyes drift shut. I was fucking tired. This week had been one exhausting day after another, and I wasn't used to trolling the bar scene anymore. I couldn't remember the last time I was out of the house at this hour.

"Sorry about this," Tiel said, her words muffled as she spoke against my shoulder.

"If you're referring to the milk, don't apologize to me about that. Don't even try," I said. "If you're referring to this wild evening, well, I'm not accepting apologies for that either. You can, however, apologize for the absolute fucking brutality of forbidding me from touching you this afternoon."

"No, I don't think I will," she said with a laugh. "Thank you for indulging me tonight."

"Anytime," I replied. "I mean that. Anytime you want to go out for the night or just have sex in the car, tell me. Between all five of my siblings, we should be able to rustle up a babysitter."

"Okay. Thank you," she repeated. "We should do this again."

"You better believe we're going to do this again. Just give me five minutes."

Then there was a knock at the window.

Tiel shrieked, and we both flinched at the bright light shining at us.

"This is going to be fun," I murmured as I rolled down the window.

The light shifted, and a police officer came into view. "Newton Police. Can I see some identification, sir?"

"Yes, of course," I replied, giving Tiel a *look what you did now* glare. "Sunshine, grab my wallet for me, would you?"

We were in the worst position for this. My trousers were in a bunched mess around my thighs, Tiel's stockings were ripped to shit, we were both covered in breast milk, and the fogged windows made it incredibly obvious that we were having more than a friendly chat back here.

She struggled to reach my back pocket without falling off

my lap. Not that I was letting that happen. *Jesus.* All we needed was my wet dick flopping around.

Once Tiel found my wallet, she handed my driver's license to the officer. I didn't know where her purse was hiding but I was certain it was out of reach, and hoped we could get by without complicating this evening any further.

The officer shined his flashlight at my identification, glancing between the card and us several times. "You took a wrong turn if you were headed for Fort Point," he said. "This is private property, Mr. Walsh."

"It is," I replied quickly. "It's *my* private property."

He gave me a dubious look and studied the darkened house for a second.

"There's a building permit on the front window," I continued. "It's in the name of Walsh Holdings, LLC. That's me. That's my firm. Tiel, get one of my business cards. There are a few in my wallet, up front."

He glanced at the card she presented and then pointed the flashlight at the windows in question but there was no way he could read it from here.

"There's also a sign on the lawn, near the mailbox, announcing this as a Walsh Associates restoration. So, yes," I conceded, "this is private property. I own it."

The officer was unimpressed. "Then you should have no trouble taking your *affairs* inside."

"We are married," Tiel cried, holding up her left hand and pointing at her rings with her right hand. "*Married.* This isn't some kind of adulterous booty call. My license is in here somewhere, and if you just turn around for a second so I can pull myself together and save you an eyeful, you can see for yourself that I'm married. To him."

I snorted out a laugh.

"No need, Mrs. Walsh," the officer said, his cheeks flushing pink. "Just don't make a habit of it. This is a family neighborhood. People here are private."

"We're heading right out," I said.

The officer nodded as he handed my license back. "You do that," he said.

"Happy holidays," Tiel called as he walked away.

I rolled the window up and stayed silent until the headlights on his cruiser pointed up the street and out of sight. Eventually, I said, "I cannot believe that just happened."

Tiel collapsed on my chest, laughing. I couldn't hold back, and laughed along with her.

"Okay, so maybe we don't do this again," Tiel said.

I shook my head. "I wouldn't go that far," I replied. "We just need to stick to properties with functioning garages."

NICK

I GLANCED down at the shiny floors and wondered how many times in the past year I'd stood in this exact spot. Fifteen, maybe twenty.

Airports carried a bittersweet flavor, one that stuck with me as long as Erin was away. I couldn't shake it until she was back in my arms and even then I struggled to choke it down. It was a byproduct of too-short weekends stretched over too-long years apart. But when I did, when I got past the taste, I remembered that wasn't our life anymore.

It was hard, Erin's travel schedule, but I wouldn't trade this life for anything. We had a place of our own, a home that was new and old all at once. She was in town more often than she wasn't, and in those moments, we were busy learning how to live together. Neither of us were particularly precious about our household habits but we'd had a few tough conversations about the right way to organize kitchen cabinets and the post-shower protocol for damp towels.

We'd put some energy into developing our dinner party muscle, and credited ourselves with bringing Alex and Riley together in the process. With Erin out of the country for the past few weeks, we had yet to invite Stremmel over. That, and he was a bull fighting the chute, too busy grousing about the weather and bemoaning the shortage of parking in Boston for me to get a word in edgewise.

Travelers spilled through the sliding doors, and I knew Erin would be soon to follow. I shifted, craning my neck to scan the crowd. People were busy tucking their passports away, pulling their phones out, looking around for car service signs.

And then I spotted her hair. It stuck out like a blazing beacon in a dark, nondescript sea. She looked up. Our eyes met across the terminal, and she raised her hand in a quick wave.

Some part of me always expected her to barrel through the terminal and leap into my arms. Or maybe we'd run toward each other. When we met, I'd pick her up and spin in dizzying circles. I didn't know why I thought that. Neither of us tended toward flamboyant gestures, and we weren't living through a romantic comedy film. But the thought crossed my mind every time I saw her emerge from Customs.

Her glasses were propped on her head, and even from this distance I could tell she was dog tired. Slumped shoulders, dark circles under her eyes, sunburned nose. The reality was that she worked too damn hard. She knew no limits when it came to studying the earth, and she put those studies ahead of everything. Herself included. And her studies weren't a matter of hard thinking in an ivory tower. She climbed volcanoes, hiked deserts, traversed miles to gather data.

Yeah, my little lovely needed a warm bed, a soft pillow, and a long rest.

As that thought crossed my mind, my cock sent up a

desperate plea. I could hear "Wait! What about my needs?" thrumming in my blood. These past weeks were the longest I could remember. The days weren't bad as I kept myself busy at the hospital, but those nights were agony. The house felt too big, too empty. I couldn't settle myself.

It was different from the time we spent apart before…well, before. I knew what it was to wake up beside her every morning now. I knew that, for all her wandering, she was a homebody at heart.

"There's always tomorrow," I said to my cock. "And all the tomorrows after that."

When Erin was within feet, I stepped toward her and lifted the backpack from her shoulders.

"Thanks for that," she said, smiling up at me.

Her rolling luggage clattered to a halt beside her, and I knew this quiet, slightly awkward reunion was better than any melodramatic run-leap-swing combination. Quiet and slightly awkward was our way.

I dropped the pack to the floor and folded her into my arms. "Anytime, Skip."

She nestled her head under my chin and, at once, we sighed. The entire world could rise and fall around us and we wouldn't notice.

"Take me home," she whispered.

Nodding, I hooked her pack over my shoulder. "I love hearing you say that," I said, my lips pressed to the crown of her head.

"Then let me say it again," she said with a grin. "Take me home, Nick."

WE COLLECTED her things and headed home to Cambridge. I drove with her hand in mine because I required that connection. She talked about her research in the Solomon Islands, and her time there. I talked surgeries, and the one-hundred-mile bike ride Matt and I took last weekend. Nothing we discussed was remarkable but it felt significant.

It was the end-of-the-day conversation I'd missed these past three weeks. The pebbles of daily life that came together to form the whole of our existence.

"I ended up next to a chatty traveler on my last flight," Erin said.

"Did this person survive the journey?" I asked. My wife's withering death stare was enough to stop most people in their tracks, but there were always a few who ignored the signs.

"Yes but barely," she said, a laugh ringing in her words. "This guy wanted to know where I was going and where I'd been. He thought he had me beat at the passport stamp game."

"Little did he know," I murmured.

"Oh yeah," she said with a smug grin. "I whipped it out and had him on his knees within two pages."

"You're starting to sound a lot like Shannon," I said. "I'm not sure how I feel about that."

"Sounds like a compliment to me." She jerked a defiant shoulder, inviting me to challenge her. I knew better than that. "When I showed him the stamps from Iceland, he ignored all the evidence suggesting that I knew something about the country and its customs because he decided to school me on holiday traditions."

"That must've been entertaining."

"It gets better," she promised. "He went on and on about the Icelandic custom of giving books on Christmas and how it dated back to medieval times. Since that's inaccurate—it started during the second World War when luxury materials were rationed but paper was not—I corrected his misconception."

"It's a public service you're doing, Skip."

"Since we were on the topic of Iceland and holidays, I figured I'd add to his knowledge base and tell him about the thirteen terrifying ogres and their evil ogre-troll mother. They climb down from the mountains every holiday season to snatch up local children. They use them for soup."

"And here I was, thinking the best part of your brain was the obscure history," I mused. "Apparently, it's Icelandic folklore."

"That story did originate in medieval times, and the children were so afraid of Grýla and the Yule Lads, they wouldn't leave their homes around Christmas."

"How did your chatty traveler respond to this?" I asked.

"He remembered that he had a newspaper to read," she replied. "My dark heart has that effect on people."

"I love you and your dark heart," I said. "Your ridiculous stories, too. Talk history to me, baby."

"During the Reformation, Oliver Cromwell and some tribalist Puritans went hard at removing the excess, decadence, and materialism from England. They canceled Christmas in 1645. That didn't last long, and Charles the Second reclaimed his seat atop the monarchy, but the sentiment stuck with the English separatists who later carried that orthodoxy across the Atlantic. Christmas was not a holiday celebrated by most seventeenth century settlers in North America. In Boston," she continued, "there were twenty-odd years when celebrating Christmas was a crime. It didn't become a federal holiday until after the Civil War."

"Ahhhh." I sighed, my palm on my chest. "I needed that. It's comfort food and foreplay, all at the same time."

"You're the only person who likes it when I dredge up this information," Erin said.

"You're the only person who can dredge up this information," I replied. "I tried to tell Hartshorn and Emmerling one of your bits of strange history, and it made no sense. You have a gift."

"Is Alex coming to Patrick and Andy's party tomorrow night?" she asked.

"She will be there, and she invited Stremmel to come along," I said as we exited Storrow Dive.

"That's interesting," Erin murmured. "Based on everything you've told me about him, I didn't expect that."

"Me neither," I said. "Hartshorn and I asked him to join us for dinner a couple of days ago. The suggestion was mildly mortifying to him."

She rubbed her thumb over the back of my hand. "He'll fit right in."

I jerked a shoulder as I pulled into our driveway. "Probably." The house was dark save for a light in the foyer. I kept her hand in mine and she followed me down the hall from the garage, into the kitchen. I stopped there, and turned to face Erin. "Are you hungry? Can I make you something?"

She shook her head and ran her knuckles down my abdomen. "I've missed you so much," she said, her words little more than a whisper. "We used to go months and months apart but now"—she looked around, her palm low on my belly—"now I can barely make it through three weeks away from you."

A breath shuddered out of me. "I know," I said. "The more of you I get, the more I want."

We stared at each other, the shadowy kitchen and our time apart fading as each second passed.

"How much of me do you want right now?" Erin asked.

Her fingers drifted to my belt buckle.

My gaze dropped to her lips.

Her pulse jumped.

My cock hardened.

"All of you," I said, grabbing a fistful of her shirt.

Tearing her clothes off the minute we walked through the door wasn't my plan, but now that I had her home, I couldn't think of anything else. I'd missed her scent, her eyes, her laugh, all of her. My lips crashed down on hers and I gathered her up in my arms.

"Upstairs," she murmured. "Bedroom."

I boosted Erin up and her legs tangled around my waist. "Best words ever spoken," I said between kisses.

"I didn't think," she whispered between quick, biting kisses, "didn't think I'd have the energy for this."

"You don't have to do anything," I promised, slamming her against coat closet door. The leverage gave me an opportunity to squeeze her ass with one hand and reach under her bra with the other. "I'll do all the work. I swear."

She was clawing at my shirt, tugging at the sides until her fingers met my skin, and I couldn't stop kissing her, biting her, growling as I rocked into her. I didn't have any words, only wants.

The stairs were so close but also so, so far.

"Upstairs," she repeated. "Bedroom. I've been roughing it for three weeks."

I tore her shirt over her head, wrenched her bra off, and sucked her breast hard. "You're kidding yourself if you think this won't be rough, lovely."

She gazed down at me, her eyes hooded, and she whispered, "Yes, please."

That was it. That was all I needed to get me moving. Clothes came off in a frantic blur, leaving a trail all the way up the stairs. It was dark and I couldn't see—didn't want to see—anything but her skin. I almost walked right past our bedroom.

"Here," Erin said, untangling her arm from around my shoulders. "This one, Nick. We don't have any furniture in the spare bedrooms yet."

I was too busy rolling her nipple around on my tongue to respond. Once I reached the bed, I set her down with as much care as I could muster. There was a balance to this. Fuck her hard, treat her soft.

Erin leaned back, her legs parting for me. "I want you right here," she said.

It hit me then how much I'd missed her. Truly missed her. "The only place I want to be."

Her heels dug into my backside in agreement, her socks warm against my bare skin as I pushed inside her. "Nick."

"Erin," I growled, my vision hazy from the flat-out pleasure of my wife in my arms and my cock buried inside her. I didn't think I could manage another word if I tried.

Her back arched off the bed as I drove into her again. Her eyes fluttered shut and her lips parted, and I brought my hand between her breasts. I wanted to own every beat of her heart, every breath. She layered both hands over mine while I stared down at her, her body quaking with my every thrust.

Her hair was tangled, her eyes were rimmed with red, her shoulders were sunburned. She was beautiful beyond belief, she was in our bed, and she was mine.

"Welcome home," I said, my lips on her neck and my heart in her hands.

LAUREN'S TEACHING staff was still small enough that they could convene meetings over French toast and huevos rancheros. She'd hired teachers who formed deep friendships and eagerly spent time together outside of work.

Audrey ran a baking blog in her spare time, and I'd already packed on five pounds from the treats that regularly came home with Lauren. Emme had a bone dry wit that somehow worked on second graders, and she knew her way around beer. I admired both of those traits. Drew and Tara were runners, and were trying their hands—feet?—at qualifying for the Boston Marathon this year. Shay was the kindest, happiest person I'd ever met, and I figured she needed that to teach kindergarten. Grace was serious and intense but she swore like a sailor after a few cocktails.

It was great, all of it. With the singular exception of my wife's sky-high red heels.

"Is that what you're wearing?" I asked. I shook my head in disbelief because no, she couldn't be leaving the house in shoes that belonged in only two locations: the bedroom and the strip club.

Lauren glanced down at her dress, tights, shoes. "I was thinking I'd wear this in the car and then pull a costume change right when we arrived at the restaurant. And then, on the way home, I'd change back into this cute Christmas-y outfit. The one I selected specifically for today's events. Would that work for you?"

I glared at the shoes again. Those things shouldn't be legal. Where did she even find them? "As long as there's a pair of reasonable shoes involved, yeah, that sounds great."

"Oh my god, Matthew," she yelled. "I love them and they're so cute. They were also on sale and that makes them ever cuter. What is your problem?"

"What's my problem? What's my *problem*?" I asked. "I hate to break it to you, Sweetness, but you can barely walk in those things. You're going to fall down stairs or trip over a crack in the sidewalk or just fall the fuck over because they're not normal shoes."

"Not this again," Lauren murmured. She studied her footwear and propped her hands on her hips. "You're going to have to reel in the caveman mania. If I want to wear heels, I'm going to wear heels. Marital compromise doesn't extend to shoes and accessories."

"I'm drawing the line at heels like those," I said, resolute.

"Oh, really?" she asked, her eyebrows arched. "You're instituting a ban on heels?"

"When they're that high, yes." I held my hands out to her. "The weather is horrendous. There's ice everywhere, and we're getting accumulating snow today and tomorrow. If you really want to wear them at the restaurant, I'll allow it but you are not wearing them on the street. I won't debate this."

"You want me to be that girl who wears Ugg boots or tennis shoes on her walk to work, and then changes into cute shoes at the office." I nodded. That was as close to accurate as we were going to get this morning. "It's like I don't even know you anymore," she said with a sigh.

"Yes, you do, Sweetness," I said, opening my arms to her. She didn't budge. "Change out of those neck-breakers and put on something that doesn't make me want to stuff your thong with cash."

Her hand settled on her belly. "I don't own any thongs, you crazy man. You really have lost your mind," she murmured. "You sound like Will sometimes."

I shook my head but she was right. Somewhat. "You might not agree with my positions," I said, nodding toward her shoes, "but I'm sure you understand my reasoning. Just take a minute to dig past your righteous indignation that I'd tell you what to do, past your dyed in the wool feminism, past your stubborn streak. When you get there, you'll find that I'm not asking for anything outrageous. I can't even breathe with how much I worry about you these days."

"Is this what you need?" She kicked off her shoes, her stocking covered feet flat on the floor. "Will this help?"

"Yes," I said at length. "Nothing matters to me but you. When are you going to believe that?"

"I do believe it, Matthew. I'll switch to flats. I'll look like a member of the Lollipop Guild but I'll do it," she said. "What else do you need?"

"I want to show you a few properties after brunch." I glanced at my watch. "You don't want to be late."

"Matthew." She spoke my name like a mild warning. "It's Christmas Eve. This isn't the day for house hunting. I have a pie to make and gifts to wrap. Additionally, we wouldn't be running late if not for this State of the Shoe address." I started to protest but she stopped me with a sharp stare. "I know you've been driving yourself to distraction over this but I promise it can wait a couple of days."

I shook my head, not deterred by her responses. "Lauren, my love, you can get off with only a banana for breakfast. You can cause me physical pain with your choices of footwear. You can even force me to keep quiet about our baby until after Shannon's kid is born," I said. "But you cannot fight me on this. Five years ago, I promised you I'd build us a house. We've waited and waited, and now it's time. I need to do this for us. For our family."

A reluctant smile pulled at the corner of her lips. "I'll get a pair of boots."

Lauren returned to the bedroom, where I heard her talking to herself in the closet. Probably going on about the ways in which my Neanderthal tendencies were driving her mad.

"They're not going to get any better," I muttered to myself.

We waited a long time to start a family. We wanted to be married for a few years and focus only on getting good at our relationship. It was a decision we arrived at together, just as we arrived at the decision to try for a baby together.

But there was one profound difference between those discussions. I knew how to be married to Lauren. I knew it the minute I met her. I didn't know how to be the father our child deserved. That left me flipping out over shoes and breathing into a paper bag every time I remembered we didn't have a proper house for our child. A home with trees to climb and pantry doors to mark my child's height every few months.

"I heard that," she said as she emerged from the bedroom, a pair of knee-high rubber rain boots on her feet.

"Was that so difficult?" I asked.

"You love it when I argue with you," she replied. "Don't pretend otherwise."

I used to think I wanted her to acquiesce to me, but I was wrong. I wanted her to meet me, inch for inch, and I wanted her to push me. I pulled, she pushed, and we found each other in the middle. It wasn't always equal, and it didn't have to be that way. Sometimes I did more of the pulling and sometimes it was mostly Lauren pushing. But the exertion made us stronger. We always came back together, and that was all I needed.

"I DON'T SEE IT," Lauren murmured, turning in a slow circle. She stared at the plywood boards over the floor, the bare studs, the crumbling fireplace. She shrugged, her lips turned down in a frown. "I want to see it. The neighborhood is nice and the yard is a good size, but...I don't see it."

It hit me then, that we'd done this before. As I thought about that day, I realized everything had changed. My entire world was different now. My father was gone, and not even his home was part of our lives anymore. My siblings were married or halfway there. I had a niece and nephew, and another on the way. And Lauren...she wasn't the same fast-talking woman who tripped down those stairs at Saint Cosmas. She was my wife. The mother of my child. My best friend. She was so much more than the sexy schoolteacher I'd met all those years ago.

"I know you see it," she continued, oblivious to the memories streaking through my mind. "You have the sight." She glanced at me, her hands burrowed deep in her coat pockets. This cold snap was fierce. "You like this one, don't you? It's your favorite of the three."

The house was a wreck but it had good, salvageable bones. An investor—probably one of those people who watched home renovation shows and thought they could pull off the same trick with fifty dollars and a weekend—had torn everything out of this 1920s farmhouse. Tore it straight down to the studs. They had enough sense to preserve the hardwood floors and some of the period details, but left a shell of a house when they ran out of money. Or know-how.

I smiled at her, nodding. "Solid foundation," I started, stepping closer, "newer roof, good systems."

Lauren waved at the empty dining room. "But no walls," she argued. "I'm fairly certain I want walls. I don't know where they'd go, but I know I want them." She turned around, sighing as she moved. "I don't know. This is just...it's a lot, Matthew."

"It is a lot but I promise you'll have walls, Sweetness," I said, laughing. "And I'll make sure they're in the right spots."

"How long will it take?" She glanced toward the living room and kitchen, both spaces dark and empty. "This looks time-intensive."

I made a *not even close* face as I shook my head. "Have I ever steered you wrong with building projects?"

"You've only steered me on one building project, Matthew," she replied. "That's not a representative sample."

"But that one came in on time and at budget," I said.

"And I'm forever grateful," she said. I pulled her close, or as close as layers of winter clothing would allow, and kissed her forehead. "If you think this is the one—"

"I do."

Lauren nodded. "I understand that you need a project right now. Some place to deposit all this expectant father energy that you're currently using on supervising my showers and agonizing over the bananas at the farmers' market."

"Some bananas are better than others," I replied. "If that's all you're going to eat for breakfast, I want to get the best banana out there."

She nodded again, as if she was taking my responses and filing them in the Totally Ridiculous But We Won't Mention That Right Now bin. "And that's why you need a project. This"—she waved her hand at the space and then pressed it to her abdomen—"feels right. For once in my life, I have no desire to plan everything or consider each possibility. If it's possible, I feel like I know what to do without thinking about it, and I want to hold onto that feeling."

"That's good because it feels right to me, too," I said.

Lauren laughed and dropped her head to my chest. "Let's do it," she said. "But you have to promise me one thing: you won't ask me to decide on every little thing for this house."

"But it's going to be our home and I want you to love it," I sputtered.

"But you restore houses every day and they're amazing. They sell for tens of millions of dollars. You know what the hell you're doing and I can't imagine where the walls go." She shot a side-eyed glance at the studs again. "Bring me in when it's time to choose paint colors and countertops, and pretty things."

She wasn't the same woman who tripped down the stairs at Saint Cosmas, and I wasn't the same man who caught her.

I pressed my forehead to hers. "This is it?" I whispered. "You're sure?"

"You think it's the one. That's all I need to know." She

nodded, brushing her lips over mine. "Just think. This time next year," she started, "our tiny person will be experiencing his or her first holidays."

That timeline hit me square in the chest. "Holy fuck, I need to get to work."

IT WAS Christmas Eve and my house looked like an active war zone.

My wife was making crazy demands fitting of a warlord. She wanted the Christmas tree stripped of its ornaments, moved to a different room, and cut six inches shorter. That was on top of rearranging the nursery this morning, cleaning out the pantry, and calling all over town to see if she could get in for a "bang trim" today. Whatever the fuck that was.

My daughter was—still—cutting teeth and chewing on anything she could get into her mouth, including chair legs and one very tolerant dog's tail. She was "helping" Shannon with her tree relocation project by yanking ornaments from the branches and tossing them to the dogs. The dogs, of course, interpreted this as a game of fetch.

My mother was simultaneously washing a million pieces of newborn clothing and linens, baking eighty-four pies, and singing off-key holiday tunes. The washing was Shannon's request, and I was damn thankful my mother was here to pick up that task but she'd turned the kitchen upside down in the process.

My father was rearranging the exterior holiday lights because I'd done it wrong. I pointed him in the direction of the ladders and staple gun without argument because last night was blessedly free from headboard banging and I knew how to pick my battles.

The military didn't prepare me for this.

"You are a precious little banshee, aren't you?" I asked, scooping my daughter up and prying a dog-slobbered ornament from her hands.

She laughed and shrieked while I lifted her like a barbell, then snuggled her into the crook of my neck. She cooed a long string of "da-da-da" and clapped her hands on my face, and I knew in my bones that the real terrorists were little baby girls with chubby cheeks and ringlets. No man alive was safe from their charms.

"Judy," I called over my shoulder. "We need you in here."

My mother bustled in from the kitchen, a flour-dusted apron tied around her waist and a swaddling blanket in her hands. "What's wrong?" she asked. "Where's Shannon? Last I saw, she was heading down to the basement. She needs to rest, Will. I haven't seen her sit down once today."

"Nothing is wrong," I said carefully. "But I need you to wrangle this cherub for a bit while I work on Shannon." I lifted Abby over my head, inciting another round of giggles. "Can you give Abby some lunch and try to get her down for a nap?"

"I'd love to," my mother said, holding out her hands for Abby. "Can you help me make pies, Miss Abigael? I'm sure you can roll some dough."

"You could also sing a little less loudly," I suggested. "Or, not at all."

"It's the holidays, Will," she said. "A few carols never hurt anyone."

I rubbed my temples and blew out a breath. I wasn't going to argue over this point. "Is Dad still outside?" I asked, glancing to the window. He'd be thrilled to handle this bullshit with the tree.

My mother huffed as she ran her fingers through Abby's white-blonde curls. "He is," she said, those two words loaded with aggravation. "I told him that if he fell off the roof and cracked his fool head open, he was driving himself to the hospital."

"That works for me." I propped my hands on my hips, nodding. "I have a few chores for him."

"Keep him off the ladders," she said, turning back toward the kitchen.

"That shouldn't be a problem," I replied.

"And keep him away from the grocery stores," she yelled from the hallway. "He always gets distracted and comes home with things we don't need."

"Roger that."

"We have ten boxes of rice pilaf in the RV," she continued, yelling from the kitchen. "Who is going to eat all that? Do y'all need any rice? We just don't have the room."

"Good on rice, Judy. Thanks."

Shaking my head, I looked down at the soggy pile of ornaments on the floor. Knowing that our child found it necessary to touch, grab, and throw everything at her level, Shannon had ordered fabric decorations for this year's tree. It saved us from cleaning up broken glass and rushing to the hospital for stitches, but now I had an armful of expensive hand-sewn chew toys.

"What the devil happened here?" my father asked.

I glared at him. Actually glared at him. He was wearing a Navy ball cap with jeans and a flannel shirt, both without a wrinkle in sight. He looked well-rested, and I didn't have any patience for that right now. Not while Shannon was probably reorganizing the entire basement or digging up that boulder she kept complaining about.

"Abby got a head start on your next project," I said.

"I'll get right on that as soon as I finish with these lights," he said.

"I'm relieving you of Christmas light duty," I said. "Shannon wants this tree moved to the family room. Make that happen. Saw a few inches off the tree, move furniture, roll up rugs, put an addition on the house. I don't care if you scrap this tree altogether and buy a new one. Do whatever you have to do, but stay off the ladders and out of the grocery stores. Understood?"

"Sir, yes sir," he replied.

I pointed to the ornaments. "Salvage as much as you can and dispose of anything you can't, but do it carefully. Leave no trace."

"I've cleaned up my share of situations," he said. "I know the standard operating procedure."

"I'm sure you do," I murmured. "I have to go find Shannon. Handle this."

My father knelt down at the base of the tree and folded the ruffly skirt. "She needs to sit down, Will," he said. "She's doing too much."

I laced my hands around the back of my neck and gazed up at the ceiling. "Yep," I said. "I'm aware of that."

He set the tree skirt—who knew that was even a thing?—on the sofa and reached up to grab the angel. "Your mother wouldn't get off her feet when she was pregnant with Wesley.

She kept running around after you and wallpapering bathrooms and baking bread, and she wouldn't listen to anyone."

"Sounds familiar," I murmured.

"Doesn't mean you should stand around with your thumb up your ass," he snapped. He was all commanding officer now, the kindly grandfather nowhere to be seen. "What the hell is wrong with you? Take care of your wife. Lay down the law if you have to."

"Thanks for the advice," I said, heading for the hall.

"I've thrown your mother over my shoulder, carried her to the bedroom and tanned her hide a time or two," he called.

"Didn't need to know that. Didn't need any of that information," I replied. "Some things are better left unsaid."

I didn't wait for his response, or another round of my mother's painfully bad singing, instead barreling down the basement stairs. Our home's underground space was one big, dark room when we moved in, like a creepy bowling alley. Now, it was segmented into his and hers storage rooms. Hers kept family heirlooms, old clothes and shoes (so many shoes), and decorations for every holiday on the calendar. Mine kept a small arsenal and a single-lane shooting range. Priorities.

I found Shannon surrounded by empty boxes, but it was the way she was staring at the heirloom section that had me worried. "Peanut," I said with a sigh. "What the hell are you doing down here?"

"This is a disaster," she said, gesturing to the shelves. Stretching up on her toes, she reached for a box labeled *Sam*. "I mean, this needs to be completely redone."

"No," I said, taking the box from Shannon's hands. "Not today it doesn't."

Shannon yanked at the box but I wouldn't give it up. "Would you rather I do it tomorrow, Will? Just get out of my way and let me sort these things. It's only going to take me fifteen minutes."

"No," I repeated. "Not happening." Her phone pinged with a notification and I plucked it from her pocket. That thing had been chiming all damn day. "I'm going to hang onto this. If anyone wants to talk to you, they need to go through me."

"Matt's buying a house," she said, waving at the phone. "I'm brokering the deal for him."

"Right now? Today?" I yelled.

"Yes, and is it really necessary to go full commando on me right now?" she asked, her hands on her hips.

"Is it really necessary to spoon-feed your brothers? Is it really necessary for you to empty every closet and storage shelf in the house?" I asked. "It will be six or seven months before this baby takes issue with the organization of the basement."

"Will, I just want this done," she said. "We're spending more time talking about it than we'll spend on doing it."

I yanked an old steamer trunk from the corner and dragged it to the least cluttered section of the room. "It will get done. Everything will be ready. I promise you," I said, backing her toward the trunk. I rested my hands on either side of her belly when she sat. "Thank you. Now, listen to me. You've done enough today. If you want something moved in here, I'll do it. I'll take care of everything you need."

"I don't need anything," she said, sighing.

I expected that. Shannon didn't walk away from an objective. Whichever target she was working toward, she hit it without incident or excuse. Even when those targets were works of homegrown nonsense.

"Sit there and tell me what to do," I said. "Pretend you're at work. Yell at me like one of your minions."

"I don't yell at anyone," she shouted. "I speak directly, and some people mistake that for yelling."

I laughed at that while I pushed the ornament boxes out of the way. "Of course you do, Peanut," I said. "Now, tell me what we're doing over here."

"First, take everything off the shelves. It's all wrong," Shannon said.

I swallowed a laugh as I reached for a box on the bottom rack. It was a good thing I loved this crazy woman.

"REMIND me again why we're doing this," I said, frowning at the dishes, produce, and chopping blocks cluttering the countertop. I moved some of it out of the way to find a seat at the kitchen island, but that earned me a pointed glare from Andy.

"I have a system here," she said, waving the spoon she was holding in the direction of the *mise en place* and me. This was what happened when I spent the morning at the gym with Sam. The goddamn kitchen exploded, or we were opening a small farmers' market. It was anyone's guess. "Please do not interrupt my system."

She pivoted, spoon in hand, and dug in the refrigerator. The absolute anarchy around us no longer mattered because the only thing I could see was her ass.

Maybe that was wrong.

Maybe I didn't care about right or wrong.

Andy was wearing candy cane knee socks, a loose gray tank top that managed to be far sexier than the slim-fitting ones she often wore, and a tiny scrap of black fabric that she called yoga shorts. I didn't know much about yoga but I knew these things were little more than underwear. I hated those shorts but I loved them more, and they were why I kept nudging the thermostat higher. Top it off with the long, thick mass of curls piled on her head, and I was ready to cancel our Christmas-Eve-meets-Hanukkah party this evening.

Cancel the whole fucking thing.

Lock the doors.

Turn off the phones.

Fuck any doubt of whether she was meant to be mine right out of her.

"Make yourself useful. Go get the wine," she said, her attention tuned to the contents of the fridge.

Look at me. See what I'm trying to tell you.

Andy and I, we didn't talk. I mean, we talked about everything. Food, work, news. But we didn't discuss big, emotional things. We didn't need to, not when we could glance at each other and communicate without speaking a word.

That worked for us. We didn't have to process every moment the way Sam and Tiel did, or insult each other all day the way Will and Shannon did, or bicker about everything the way Matt and Lauren did. We made it through with nods and arched eyebrows and smirking smiles. That was enough.

Except when it wasn't enough.

We weren't making it through right now. I needed her words. There'd been a few instances when I'd needed them before. After Riley had found us seconds away from christening my desk at the office, all those years ago. When I thought it was over and I'd be forced to live out my days as a crabby curmudgeon who got drunk off the scent of lavender. When she'd been so, so sick with an aggressive case of food poisoning that morphed into a blood infection and her body started shutting down, and the possibility of losing her hung over me like a dense fog.

And now, when it seemed we'd drifted far off course. I needed more than her murmurs and small smiles. I needed to know we were still on this journey together, and I needed to know where we were going.

"Is there a reason you're strangling the merlot?" Andy asked. I blinked at her from across the kitchen island. "You've been staring at those bottles—and gripping them like you're trying to break them—for a few minutes."

"No," I replied, scowling at the wine. "Just…thinking."

"About merlot?"

"About you," I said honestly.

Her eyes widened and the mixing spoon in her hand stilled. "Care to elaborate?"

I stared at Andy for a moment, then the bottles, and then back at her. That hair. That fucking hair did it to me every time. Those curls made my fingers itch. I wanted to tug it all loose and dig my fingers through those strands.

I wanted that to be enough. I wanted to tell her everything with that one move, and all the moves that would follow. I wanted her to read my mind now, like she always did, and know exactly what I required from her.

Maybe that would work. My hands in her hair, her body beneath mine, no conversation required. That would work. I could drag her into the bedroom and solve this—no. *No.* That didn't solve my problems yesterday. Not my biggest problems, of course.

"Perhaps you could finish unpacking the wine while you glare at me," Andy said. "Or do you need to devote all of your energy to the glaring?"

I set the bottles down and freed two more from the box. "Satisfied?" I plunked another two on the counter.

"Hm," she murmured, turning away from the island.

"Why are we doing this?" I repeated, grabbing an avocado from the countertop and scowling at it.

"Because I like having people over," she said. She had that one eyebrow, the one that always gave me the business, arched all the way up. "I *like* having dinner parties, and having holiday traditions. I *like* cooking for everyone, but you already know that."

Somewhere along the way, my quiet girl with her "hm" and bent eyebrow and private smiles turned into the Hostess with the Most-ess. And she did, she enjoyed this. It was fascinating and delicious, and occasionally exhausting. But now, before everyone invaded our home, I was past the point of exhausted. More than that, I was past the point of needing uninterrupted time with her.

I didn't want to spend the night surrounded by people who were not my fiancée. Or wearing pants. I'd had enough with pants for this year.

I set the avocado down with more force than the fruit deserved. "*I* don't like having people over."

"You always say that," Andy said. "But then you enjoy it, and you say we should do it more often."

She pointed the spoon at me. "It's also Christmas Eve and the last night of Hanukkah. You can deal for this short time, Patrick."

I could. I could even enjoy it. It had all the makings of an incredible night. Shannon and Will were going out for— presumably—the last time before the baby arrived. Erin was home for the holidays. Riley was testing out some new cock- tails on us. Ellie was staying at the firehouse with baby Dave to give his parents the night off. These were all good things, and I could absolutely deal with one night of friends and family.

But I didn't *want* to deal.

I pointed at the stovetop. "What's the story there? Are you watching the pot, or will it stay for a bit?"

"Don't start," she said, circling the spoon in my direction. "I have a system. I have a timeline. I love you, but don't start right now."

"You have plenty of time to finish whatever the fuck you're doing with all this food—"

"The menu," Andy interrupted, her tone as frosty as the winter wind in Boston, "is on the refrigerator. You may recall that I discussed it with you last night, too."

I stared at the strong line of her back and the way she appeared to set six different things in motion at once. Chopping cucumbers, rinsing lettuce, pulling olives from the refrigerator, assembling an artful cheese board. I was about to start smashing these bottles. Just throwing them down and watching them shatter as they hit the hardwood floor, the dark red liquid rushing out like blood from a wound. Anything to get her attention back.

But then she popped a bit of crumbly cheese into her mouth and I had a hundred tiny heart attacks. "Where is that from?" I asked, rounding the island. I yanked her wrist away from the tray and licked the remnants from her fingertips.

"The cheese place Shannon likes. The one in Chestnut Hill," Andy replied. "I went there after the lingerie shop."

She shot me a sharp smile, the kind that said *Remember when you did filthy things to me in a dressing room? When you almost fucked me through the wall?*

"Don't try to distract me," I growled, my brows knitting together.

She dropped her free hand to my chest and rubbed, as if she could loosen the tension I was carrying with her touch. And she could. "It's simple old goat cheese. Nice and pasteurized. No scary bacteria to be found, and it's been more than a year and a half since my run-in with the overly funky cheese," she said lightly. "I'm okay. Raw fish, runny eggs, soft cheese, they're all fine. *I'm* fine."

She was fine, and I knew that, but it was times like these when I felt her slipping away from me that turned up all my irrational desires to keep her close, keep her safe. It didn't matter that my opponents were questionably aged dairy products and middle-aged women rebelling against the patriarchy. It was how I felt, and as Lauren liked to say, everyone was allowed to feel their feelings.

"I know," I said, tugging her against me. "But I worry. I'm going to do it, and you're going to deal with it."

"I accept that," she said. "But I also want you to believe I'm not going anywhere."

We weren't talking about cheese anymore. We couldn't be. "Are you sure about that?"

"Certain," she replied with a laugh. Maybe we were talking about cheese. I didn't fucking know. I didn't know anything. "How I can leave when you're so busy glaring at me?"

I ran my hand down her spine and pressed her hips closer, until she was flat against me. "You enjoy my glaring."

"So much," she replied. "Are you going to tell me what you were thinking about? Or is that another one of your mysteries?"

"Where is your ring?" I asked, running the pad of my thumb over the empty spot on her finger.

She tipped her chin toward the open shelves on the other

side of the kitchen. "In the jar right up there," she said. "I took it off before I tossed the vegetables in marinade."

"Is that the only reason?"

Her forehead crinkled and her eyes narrowed as she studied me. "What are you asking me?"

I was ready. I had it teed up and I was going to lay it all out for her now. It didn't matter that we were expecting a horde of guests in half an hour. This was the right moment. Now. This was it. I was going for it. "I think we need to talk about—"

The door banged open and Riley's voice rang out. "I've finally figured it out," he called.

"Why does this always happen?" Andy whispered, her shoulders rocking with laughter.

"Don't you want to know?" he asked. "Don't give me that face, Optimus."

"Know what?" I roared. "How the fuck you got in? Because I'm really fucking curious about that right now."

Riley rolled his eyes. "You gave me a key three years ago. When you guys went to Scotland."

"And somehow you decided this was the right moment to use it," Andy murmured, her head still tucked under my chin. I brought my hand to the back of her neck, my fingers sliding into her hair.

"I thought you'd want to hear about the holiday cocktails I created for your shindig." He moved a case of liquor to the countertop, beside the wine. "But—apparently—that's not one of your priorities."

"It really isn't," I said.

At the same time, Andy asked, "What's the drink?"

"The first one I'm calling the Honeybee. It's angostura bitters for heat, honey syrup for sweet, lemon juice for tart, and a mezcal rinse for smoke. And tequila. Lots of tequila." He shrugged. "It's mostly tequila."

"People are going to be having sex in our house, aren't they?" Andy asked under her breath.

"No," I replied, shaking my head. "We'll kick them out before it gets to that point. They'll have sex in the hallway."

"That's only slightly better than a dressing room," she said, a laughing ringing in her words.

I slipped my hand down the back of her shorts and squeezed her ass. "I didn't hear you complaining yesterday."

"I doubt you heard anything over all those growls of yours," she said, sliding her hand under my shirt and up my back.

"The second one," Riley started, his voice booming as he talked over us, "I'm calling the Frisky Whiskey. It's blood orange juice, lemon juice, agave, orange bitters, and Amaro. It's a bittersweet Italian digestif."

"Any whiskey?" Andy asked. "Since it's part of the name."

"Oh, right," he replied. "Yeah, a ton of whiskey. Like, ninety percent whiskey, ten percent everything else. I would classify both of these drinks as Grade A Panty Droppers."

"You know how some people tell stories about being house-bound during snowstorms and hurricanes, and how there's a baby boom nine months later?" I asked. Andy murmured in agreement. "We're going to be blaming Riley's signature drinks for the next baby boom."

Andy shifted in my arms and grinned at Riley. "I hope you know what you're doing."

"Of course I do," he replied, pulling fruit and bottles from his box. "Where do you want me to set up?"

"How about you go for a walk around the block and come back in half an hour?" I asked. "Think up another drink."

"Something with vodka and cherries. Something strong enough to make me giggle," she suggested.

"I'm defenseless when you're giggly," I said, squeezing her backside with each word. "I fuckin' love it."

"I know," she replied, her eyes bright and her smile wide.

"Goddamn it, you two." Riley set a bag of lemons down and shook his head at us. "This is unacceptable. You need to manage your time better," he said. "If you want to get freaky, you don't wait until a few minutes before your party."

"Thank you for that pearl of wisdom, RISD," Andy said.

"You're very welcome." He reached for a dish of olives and helped himself to a handful. One of them slipped out of his grip and rolled across the kitchen floor. He didn't notice. "Besides, Alex is in surgery for another hour or two so you're stuck with me. I'm going to hang out here and squeeze some citrus. If you're lucky, I'll mix up a Nip Slip just for you, Andy."

"It's probably unwise to ask this," I started, "but what is in a Nip Slip?"

"Vodka, grenadine, vodka, orange curaçao, vodka," he replied, rambling off the ingredients as he organized his items. "And two cherries."

"That will do just fine," Andy said. "Will you make me a Bloody Mary tomorrow morning, too?"

"Sure," he replied easily. "Just as long as you don't mind coming to Alex's apartment for it, or me mixing drinks in my nakeds."

"We'll skip the nakeds," I said. "Thanks."

"I noticed that the other apartment on this floor is for sale," Riley said. "Wouldn't it be cool if Alex and I moved in there? We could be neighbors and you could come over for Bloody Marys all the time."

"That's not going to happen," I snapped.

"It could," Riley argued.

"No." It wasn't happening because I bought that apartment yesterday. "It's under contract."

"That was fast," Andy said.

This didn't deter Riley. I wasn't certain anything deterred my youngest brother. "I'll have to watch the units downstairs, then."

"Or you could live somewhere else," I suggested. "Anywhere else, actually."

Andy turned back to face me, locking her arms around my waist in the process. "Wasn't there something you wanted to talk about?" she asked, tipping her head toward Riley. "What were you saying? Before the interruption?"

I gazed down at her, taking in her dark eyes, full lips, flawless skin. "Nothing that can't wait until later."

I'D BEEN TRYING to weasel out of this event all day but between Hartshorn and Emmerling, I had no hope. They had me cornered, and they weren't letting me off easy. I tried picking up a hot appendix, but Hartshorn handed the case off to a resident and ordered me to change out of my scrubs.

Fuck my life.

I didn't know anyone at this party aside from the GI hottie, who I adored primarily because she was unavailable and that was my kryptonite. Also, on my second day at the hospital, she told me where to get a life-altering gyro and she wasn't wrong. It did change my life.

Aside from the woman of my unattainable dreams, I only knew Hartshorn and Acevedo, and the GI hottie's boyfriend. I didn't exactly *know* him. We just traded glares in the hallway.

Hartshorn rapped his knuckles on my locker in the attending surgeons' lounge. "Let's get a move on," he said. "Emmerling will catch up with us later."

"Forgive me," I started, gesturing to him. The guy was like a goddamn boulder. I didn't understand how he had the dexterity to work on hearts. "But where the hell are we going? And who are these people?"

He moved his shoulders in the type of shrug that clearly communicated his disinterest in replying. "Acevedo's in-laws. Basically," he said. "They're good people and they always have good food and drink." He gestured to me, indicating that I was to finish dressing. "It'll be fine. Come on."

I figured the guy was going to be Chief of Surgery soon enough, and I'd better do as I was told. I didn't have it in me to fuck up another gig, and as much as I hated the cold weather, I tolerated this hospital.

Tolerance was as close as I could come to enjoying anything these days.

No. No, that wasn't right. I enjoyed the hell out of that GI surgeon. That woman knew how to wear a pair of scrubs, my god. And she was fucking nice to me. *Nice.* To *me.* No one had been intentionally nice to me since Christ was a carpenter.

But since the world hated me, the GI surgeon had a boyfriend, and that guy made a point of stabbing me with his eye daggers every time our paths crossed. He knew what I was thinking when I looked at her, and he didn't appreciate those thoughts. That should've given me pause. Forced me to reflect on my behavior. It didn't.

"You're sure about this?" I asked as I shoved my arms into a shirt. "Seems strange for me to crash a family event."

He stared at his pager, frowning. "They won't mind. It's a big group."

"Yeah, sure," I murmured. "I'll just blend in. That always works."

"They won't mind if you sit in the corner feeling sorry for yourself all night," he added.

It wasn't clear whether he was speaking from experience or commenting on my general demeanor. Probably both.

"Uh," I murmured, holding my hands out as I feebly gestured to the jeans and plaid shirt I'd worn to the hospital before changing into scrubs this morning. I wasn't one of those docs who could wear a suit under my white coat. A day didn't go by without getting a considerable amount of bodily fluids on my scrubs. That was the nature of trauma and emergency work. If it wasn't messy, it wasn't my service.

"They won't notice," he said. He was decked out in a red flannel shirt that made him look like Saint Nick's hipster brother.

"Am I supposed to bring anything?" I asked. I was desperate now. Any reason to bail, I was taking it.

"I was supposed to bring Emmerling," he said, rubbing the back of his neck. "But she was called into that septic gallbladder."

"Maybe we should wait for her," I suggested. "How long is a septic gallbladder going to take anyway? She'll be done within twenty minutes. Out of post in thirty."

"You don't see many septic gallbladders, do you?" he asked, pulling a scarf around his neck. I shook my head. "She'll be in there for an hour. Maybe two. She said to go on without her."

"You're sure? Really? I don't think we should show up to a family thing empty-handed *and* missing Emmerling."

I sounded like a whiny bitch. *I am a whiny bitch.*

"We're good," he said, waving toward the door. "They won't mind. Come on."

We headed from the hospital toward the neighborhood where this party was taking place, the North End. I didn't know much about this city or how to navigate the impossibly narrow one-way streets. I had no problem with walking, either, but it was too damn cold for this shit.

Cal pointed us in the right direction, occasionally stopping to explain the significance of one location or another. Monuments, squares, memorial bridges. I wasn't here for the history lesson but I nodded along as if I was studying up for the final exam.

We procured a nice bottle of champagne at the Public Market since I kept harassing Hartshorn about bringing something. We agreed champagne was universally appreciated, but Cal made some snarly noises when I tried to pay. He got over it pretty quickly and resumed with his tour guide routine.

"You really like this city," I said after a long speech about a molasses flood that happened a hundred years ago. I shoved my hands into my pockets, searching for a corner of warmth to fight off the fucking horror of this wind chill. I had few happy memories of Los Angeles at this point but I didn't appreciate the weather while I had it. Even the crazy-hot days when it seemed like the LA Basin was going to melt right into the ocean.

"I do," Hartshorn agreed. He didn't seem to notice the weather. Maybe he didn't see a reason to complain about everything in the entire world the way I did. "It was an adjustment for me, too. But after I stopped adjusting and started living, I found this is a nice place to call home."

I grunted out something that sounded like an agreement and kept my head down. Part of me couldn't believe I'd been conscripted into this friends-of-friends holiday catastrophe. I did not do this shit. I didn't meet up with people from the hospital for a few beers or join the department's kickball league.

Then again, I wasn't invited to join those events with any frequency.

But the other part of me knew that I would've been sitting at home, alone, alternately eating beef lo mein and jerking off to the college cheerleading championship on ESPN. That sounded infinitely better than socializing. Those chicks were so fucking flexible. Tough, too.

"Are there going to be any women at this thing?" I asked.

Hartshorn bobbed his head. "Yeah, of course. There's always a big group."

"Okay. Good. Good to hear." I nodded several times and forced myself to feel better about this. "So, you're the head of cardio-thoracic surgery and you don't get the holidays off? That doesn't motivate me to advance," I asked, aiming for jokey and collegial but sounding like a prick.

I am a prick. The biggest fucking prick.

"I take long weekends here and there," he said. "I'd rather work the holidays and let the surgeons with kids and families have the time off. Doesn't bother me."

This guy was a fucking saint. I couldn't even stand it.

"My mom's a physician," he continued. "She's the only doc in something like two hundred square miles. Rural Oregon. Her practice is mostly clinic hours and house calls. The holidays aren't a sacred day when that's your life, so it doesn't bother my family that I'm not home." He shot me a quick glance. "What about you? Are you from California originally?"

I jerked my shoulder in response, but the bulk of my coat obscured it. Fucking winter. "I'm from central Florida. That boring part, not the touristy part."

He glanced over at me. "Do you get back there often?"

"No."

"Can't imagine the holidays in Florida are much like this." Hartshorn waved at the icy patches on the sidewalk.

"They're not."

I left it at that. This guy was a saint and he'd be my boss one of these days, but I didn't need to drop my dirty laundry and daddy issues at his feet. Just because he gave me a glimpse into his complex inner life didn't mean I had to return the favor. I didn't do that kind of heart-to-heart shit with anyone.

People said that made relating to me difficult. That I was defensive and unapproachable. I said I didn't give a fuck. Pediatricians and dermatologists needed to be approachable. The only things people really wanted from their trauma surgeon was an ability to think fast and keep them alive, and since I did both of those things with success, I was sticking with unapproachable. Defensive, too. Anyone who had a problem with it could go fuck themselves.

"Is that where your family lives?" he asked. "Florida?"

"Some," I grunted. "I don't see much of them or the Sunshine State anymore."

My parents split when I was little. Before kindergarten. My father invented as-seen-on-TV shit, and was on the never-ending hunt for his next big thing. That was his first and only love, and that was fine by me. My mother remarried when I was a teenager. A rich, real estate dickhead. Aside from the fact I could count on him to snag Super Bowl tickets on the regular, I had no use for the guy.

"I could go for some warmer weather," Hartshorn said with a chuckle. Seriously, Saint Nick's brother. "But, hell, I like it here. Acevedo and Emmerling are family to me."

"That's nice." I meant it amiably but I couldn't say anything without broadcasting my status as the city's biggest douche.

"It is," he agreed. If he noticed my prick tone, he ignored it. "None of us get much time together outside the hospital but I'm thankful for them. And Acevedo's wife, and her family. They're good people, good friends."

"Mmhmm."

I didn't make friends. I was the bull in the china shop, breaking everyone and everything until someone got the tranq gun and took me down. They always kicked my sedated ass to the curb. I traded on my surgical skills, and not much else. It was a goddamn blessing that I was exceedingly capable in the operating room.

"They're a little mad but the best ones are," Cal said, laughing to himself again. He stopped and glanced up at an old brick building. I still couldn't get over how old everything was here. "This is it. Pretend I didn't drag you here against your will."

"Didn't you though?" I asked under my breath.

"Call it mandatory team building," he replied with a grin. He was just too fucking jolly for real life.

I heard the party as soon as we rounded the landing to the third floor. The door was propped open with an ice chest full of beer bottles. It was high quality beer, too. Maybe this wasn't going to be so bad.

"Cal," a man just inside the door called. "Good to see you, man. Wasn't sure you'd make it."

He pulled Hartshorn in for a one-armed hug-back-clap move. "You too, Sam," Hartshorn replied. He gestured to me. "Stremmel, this is Sam Walsh. Sam, Sebastian Stremmel, our newest trauma surgeon. We stole him from UCLA."

That was barely accurate but I wasn't saying shit about my last gig.

"Los Angeles, huh," he said, studying my brand-new winter coat. "This cold snap must be killer."

"You have no idea," I said as I turned and shrugged off the outerwear.

"Wanted to ask you about qualifying for the Boston Marathon," Hartshorn said to Sam.

"Are you thinking about running it?" Sam asked.

"Hell no," Hartshorn replied with a deep laugh. "I max out on half-marathon runs. I have no interest in twenty-six miles, but there's a resident on my service who wants to give it a shot."

I surveyed the space and stepped away, trying to drop out of their discussion without arousing notice. Music was playing low enough to keep the conversation flowing. Groups congregated near the fireplace, the tree, the bar where Emmerling's boyfriend was pouring drinks, and the wide doors leading to the dark terrace. Instead of merging into those groups or taking Hartshorn's advice and finding a corner in which to sulk, I moved toward the open kitchen.

A dark-haired beauty stood at the island, her hands busy with an array of dishes spread out before her. She was gorgeous and graceful, and I should've snatched the champagne from Hartshorn before coming over here because I couldn't approach a woman this far out of my league without a sacrificial offering in hand.

It was too late for that now. I was going in unarmed, but that didn't lessen my chances of success. I was fucking awesome when it came to situations with the worst odds. I was meant for that shit.

"Merry Christmas." I sidled up to the island, smiling. "You must be the hostess."

She glanced up at me, her eyebrow arched and her expression anything but merry. "I suppose that's accurate," she said, her tone cool. "And who must you be?"

"Stremmel," I replied, holding my hand out to her. "Sebastian Stremmel."

She offered my outstretched hand a glimpse but didn't stop whisking. "Hands full," she said, tipping her chin toward the stainless steel bowl in front of her.

I didn't know what the hell she was making but I appreciated the force she put into the task. From the looks of it, she could bring me to my knees, kick my ass, and then demand I thank her for the opportunity. And I wasn't opposed to any of that.

"You're living in Nick's old apartment, right?" she asked.

Her words snapped me out of my filthy thoughts and I stuck my hand in my pocket. "Right," I murmured. Acevedo's apartment was sacred ground. The guy was some sort of legend. Twenty years from now, it would still be known as Acevedo's apartment.

She held up the whisk, frowning. "These aren't stiff peaks," she announced. "Why aren't these stiff peaks?"

I meant to look at the whisk. I really did. But I stared at her breasts instead. "Yeah, I—hmm." Her black v-neck sweater was heaven-sent, and the hint of cleavage at the apex was worth every minute of this friends-of-friends holiday catastrophe. "I don't know."

She sprinkled something into the mixture and resumed her whisking. There was no way to watch this without dreaming of hand jobs. No fucking way.

"You're a surgeon, right? What's your specialty?"

"Trauma," I said. I sensed someone watching me and hooked a glance over my shoulder. Emmerling's boyfriend was doubled over laughing while a man I hadn't noticed until now was staring at me. He was scowling, his arms crossed over his chest. I didn't know what any of that was about and didn't exactly care. "Hey." I nodded at him. He didn't respond, so I turned back to my pretty new hostess friend. "What do you do, sweetheart?"

"Architect," she replied, her attention fully tuned to her whisk and the uncooperative ingredients.

"That's interesting. Not a profession I hear about every day," I said, smiling. "Thank you for accommodating the last minute addition. I hope I'm not imposing."

She tapped the whisk on the edge of the bowl, seemingly pleased with the peaks, and waved me off. "No trouble," she said, sliding the bowl in the refrigerator. "You know what they say. The more the merrier."

I'd never known that to be true but I wasn't arguing with the pretty lady. The pretty lady who wore a grand total of zero rings.

"What's your name, hostess?"

There was a noise behind me, almost a growl, but I ignored it. She pinned me with another cool glance, the type that warned me off and reeled me in all at once. She was going to make me work for every scrap, and I respected that.

"My fiancée's name is Andy."

A riotous laugh went up behind me. I tore my gaze away from the hostess and watched a man—the one with the scowl —join her behind the island. A groan started in my toes and worked its way up, stopping at each vital organ to gain size and speed until I was muttering "Fuck" for a full minute.

"Sebastian," Andy with the fiancé started, "this is Patrick." She gestured between me and the man who was planning how he'd kill me tonight. "Patrick, this is Sebastian. He lives in Nick's old apartment."

"Welcome to *our* home," Patrick said, each word rougher than the one before. His hand moved from Andy's shoulder down her back. If the widening of her eyes was any indication, he was giving her ass one hell of a pinch. "Get a drink. Have a bite. Make yourself comfortable. Never speak to my fiancée again."

Another laugh sounded from over my shoulder, and I shifted to find the guests watching with fascination. Emmerling's boyfriend was chuckling behind his fist and I'd never wanted to beat his ass more than I did right now. Beat his ass and then disappear because I wasn't used to getting shot down with a captive audience.

"Put your ring back on," Patrick said, his forehead tipped against Andy's temple and his lips lingering over her ear. I wasn't meant to hear any of this but I couldn't stop watching them. "You torture me, Kitten."

"I don't mean to," she purred, her lips pulled up in a grin.

Oh, she fucking meant it. Meant every damn minute.

"Yes, you do," he said. "Perhaps I should steal you away and explain it better."

She shook her head. "I'm watching the paella. You'll have to save the lecture for later."

He dragged the shell of her ear between his teeth. "You can believe I will."

I needed to duck away from this exchange and get the fuck out of here. My bed and those cheerleaders sounded damn good right about now. Before I could calculate my next move, a whirlwind of a redhead blew in.

"Oh my god, Andy, there was so much traffic," she said. "I thought I was going to waste away on the drive here. Where do you want these? Judy made them so they're amazing but I want you to keep them away from me. If I see them, I'll eat them all. I had ten on the ride here. Maybe twenty. I lost track. And don't let me near the paella either. I'm maxed out on spice and I can't stomach another chalky antacid tablet."

She was talking a mile a minute and carrying a large platter of cookies but none of that caught my attention. It was cleavage on display like sweet holiday hams. I could get lost between those babies. Suffocate and die happy.

"Hello," I drawled. "You have your hands full there. Can I help you with that?"

I gestured to her platter but she only glanced to Andy and Patrick with a quizzical look. Andy shook her head, shrugging, and Patrick was still figuring out how he'd dispose of my body.

"No, I've got it," she sang. "I know my way around a handful. Thanks, though. You're a peach."

"We're calling this peach Sebastian," Andy said. "He's very special. I think you two are really going to hit it off."

"What's your name, doll?" I asked, leaning closer to her. "I'm writing my naughty and nice lists. Wouldn't want to forget you."

"Put me down for naughty. All the way." She smiled and there was warmth behind it, but it also scared me. She gave me the impression that she'd be amazing in bed but she might also snap off my dick in the process. "Shannon Halsted. The naughtiest. Number one naughty girl."

"You're looking for so much trouble, Shannon," Andy said with a laugh.

"You started the trouble," Patrick said to Andy.

"The only trouble I have is with my whipped cream." She rearranged the dishes on the countertops around her. "Let me make some space and I'll take those cookies. We'll see what happens then. This can only get more interesting."

"And by interesting," Patrick said, "you mean likely to end in bloodshed."

Ignoring them, I edged closer and wrapped my fingers around Shannon's elbow. "How does an angelic woman like yourself earn the title of number one naughty girl?"

"I pray someone is recording this," Patrick muttered.

Three things made themselves clear when the tray shifted from the redheaded whirlwind to the pretty dark-haired lady. One, the ring on Shannon's finger made it clear she was married. No mistaking the wedding band. Two, she was pregnant. Massively pregnant. Her skin-tight purple dress—the one that put her breasts out there like a damn headline— allowed no mysteries.

"What the actual fuck is going on here?" a voice thundered from behind me. The voice belonged to a man who had—at a minimum—fifty pounds of muscle on me. His button-down shirt was stretched across his arms and chest, and his hands were opening and closing into fists.

And three, I was going to get my ass handed to me at least once tonight. Then, Hartshorn and I were going to have a lengthy discussion about the right way to set expectations.

Shannon gestured toward me, her eyes sparkling. Yeah, she'd take a bite out of me. "This is Sebastian."

It sounded more like, *This is the dead bird the cat left on the doorstep.*

"He's a peach," Patrick added.

That sounded like, *He's a fucking dickhead.*

They weren't wrong about any of it.

"Step away from my wife," the husband said as he moved toward me. His hand landed on my wrist and yanked me away from Shannon's elbow. "You will not touch her again."

I wasn't a weak guy. I could handle more than my share of

pressure and pain. But the grip this man had on my wrist was testing all of that. And he hadn't blinked once.

"Be nice, Commando," Shannon said to him.

Acevedo stepped between us, his coat still zipped and hat pulled low over his ears, and he shot a warning glance in my direction. "I'll take it from here, Will."

After a heavy pause, Will released my wrist. He, too, was busy thinking up ways to dismember me.

"Let's head outside," Nick said, his palm flat on my chest. "We need to have a little chat."

I followed him out of the apartment and down the hall. I should've grabbed my coat on the way because I was definitely getting the boot. From this party, these people, and probably this hospital. It was a good thing I hadn't unpacked yet.

When we reached the far end of the hall, Acevedo turned to face me. His hands were braced on his hips and he didn't say anything. Not a goddamn word. He stared at me the way a parent stared at an out of line child while waiting for an admission of guilt.

Since I wasn't one to admit a fucking thing even when surrounded by a literal shit-ton of evidence, I studied the old photographs on the walls. Apparently this building was home to a pasta factory back in the day—many, many days ago—and the residents wanted a daily reminder of that history.

I didn't understand this city.

"Let me give you some advice," Acevedo said, clapping my shoulder. "Turn it down. This isn't ladies' night at the bar, okay? Aside from the fact these women are married or otherwise unavailable, they're my friends. This isn't a meat market."

"I asked Hartshorn if there'd be women here," I argued. "He said yes."

"Yeah, well, Hartshorn is really fuckin' linear," Acevedo

said with a shrug. "He's also in love with a woman he's never spoken to, so he doesn't think like a single guy."

"That's complicated," I muttered.

"Truly." He nodded, rolling his eyes a bit. As if I didn't know the half of it. I didn't. People never told me their stories or shared personal shit. I was too busy being unapproachable.

I pointed toward the door. "Should I just go? Would that be better?"

Acevedo shook his head as he dipped his hands into his pockets. "No, you're not doing that," he said. "Just do both of us a favor and leave the women alone if you can't mute the pick-up lines. Halsted will actually kill you if that doesn't stop."

I laughed but the sharp glint in his eyes shut me right up.

"He's a former Navy SEAL. He owns a private security firm now. The guy has connections," Acevedo said. "He's also extremely protective. Andy, Shannon, and his sister Lauren—you haven't smarmed all over her yet—went out to a club a few years ago. They wanted to go dancing and we all went along because what else would we do? A few drunk guys wouldn't leave them alone. Will dragged all five of these guys out of the club *at once* and whipped the tar out of them. By himself. He didn't have a drop of blood on him and I don't think he broke a sweat."

I ran my hands through my hair. "Oh, shit."

Acevedo pulled his pager from his pocket and studied it for a moment. "He has a crossbow in his basement. He let me shoot it once."

"Oh, shit," I repeated. "He will actually kill me."

"Yeah, he will," Acevedo replied. He tipped his head toward me, pausing. "You know, it shouldn't require the threat of a woman's husband gravely injuring you to leave her alone.

If she's not interested, you could back off. It's a matter of basic respect."

"Don't give me the respect lecture, man. I respect women plenty."

"Seems debatable," he murmured.

"It was a misunderstanding. I'm not one of those guys." I rubbed my temples and stared at the floor. It was old hardwood, scarred and battered. I felt that. Every dark mark in the glossy golden wood mirrored my roughly patched spots. "This is why I don't do things with people from work," I grumbled.

"Because someone will call you on your bullshit?" Acevedo asked.

"No," I said, finally meeting his eyes. "Because I fuck shit up. I'm not good with people or—you know—anything that isn't surgery. I didn't want to come here tonight, but Hartshorn dragged me by the ear. I was going to stay at home, or hang around the hospital and pick up procedures because I have no business at events like this."

Acevedo regarded me for a long moment. "No, dude. You're in the right place."

I had a salty response ready but it died as I turned his words over in my head. "What the hell does that mean?"

He jerked a shoulder up. "It means you should come inside with me. You're in good company," he said. "I don't think many of them make a habit of hitting on married women, but they have their own quirks." I gave him a dubious stare and he laughed. "Come on. Andy made paella. Do you like paella?"

"I—uh—I don't know," I replied. "I don't think I've ever had paella."

"You'll like it," he said. "The rice on the bottom gets nice and crispy. It's the best part."

"You want me to stay," I said, "and eat crispy rice."

"Yes," he said, nodding.

"After everything that just happened."

"Yes," he repeated. Still nodding.

"I don't understand this city," I murmured.

"You don't have to," he replied. "We'll eat, we'll drink, we'll reminisce about the days when we were young and naïve and the world wasn't a dumpster fire. Just stop trying to pick up the ladies and they'll adopt you before the end of the night."

My lip curled into a scowl. I was thirty-eight years old and I'd managed well enough without any form of family for nearly two decades. "That's the last thing I need."

Acevedo scratched his chin as he stared off into the distance for a moment. "There was a time when I thought the same thing," he said. "I was wrong about that, and a lot of other things, too." He started back toward the apartment, glancing at me over his shoulder. "Come on. We'll get you one of Riley's drinks and you'll forget any of this ever happened."

"He'll probably dip his balls in it," I grumbled.

"I wouldn't doubt it," Acevedo replied. "But like I said, we'll feed you enough liquor to make you forget all of this."

ACEVEDO WAS right about the crispy rice. The drinks, too. And Hartshorn was right about sitting in the corner and sulking. I needed all of those things to keep myself from floating away on a river of resentment and bitterness tonight. It helped that I had an unobstructed view of Emmerling once she arrived, and plenty of time to admire her while the boyfriend snarled at me.

My drinks were definitely garnished with a hint of testicle but it was too easy to fuck with that guy. Too damn easy.

Acevedo was right about these people, too. They gave me my share of shit for hitting on a pregnant woman, and once I climbed out of my hole from those unfortunate choices, I could see some of the humor. Despite the rocky start and my tremendous desire to hate everything, they were welcoming. With the exceptions of Patrick and Will—they were still working on that death and dismemberment plan—I had easy conversations with everyone. Lauren and I talked about Southern California. Emmerling offered up hospital gossip and some taqueria recommendations. Matt invited me to join him for a run or bike ride. Sam and I debated college football. Erin promised to have me over for dinner after the holidays.

I couldn't hate any of this, and I'd tried.

They engaged in the most bizarre form of gift-giving I'd ever witnessed, something they called a Yankee Swap. It looked an awful lot like a Manifest Destiny land grab with liquor. There were numbers drawn from a mixing bowl, wrapped bottles lined on the coffee table, and an illogical system for selecting an unopened bottle or stealing one from someone else. They forced me to participate, and I was now the owner of every teenage girl's alcohol of choice, Goldschläger. I figured it would pair well with college cheerleaders and my left hand.

Hartshorn scrolled through his phone, sighing and murmuring as he went. "Why don't we head out?" he asked, still scrolling. "I want to check on my post-ops."

"Don't do that," Emmerling said. She looked like a fucking prize in those jeans. "You have residents for that."

"She's right," Acevedo said from the sofa. He swung his arm around Shannon's shoulder and tugged her close. Evidently, he was permitted to snuggle the SEAL's wife. I had questions but I wasn't asking them. "Let us suggest a tavern where you two can drink your sorrows away."

"I don't have any sorrows," Hartshorn replied, his expression stony. "I'm filled with joy."

"Brimming," Emmerling said. I was staring at her thighs, imagining how they'd feel as earmuffs. "Overflowing, even. We can barely handle all your joy."

"Head down to Sullivan's. Sit at the bar. Order whiskey. Be miserable and hate the world," Shannon said, wagging a finger between us. "You might feel terrible tomorrow but I can promise you that being miserable at Sullivan's on Christmas Eve is the path to good things."

"I'm not miserable," I lied, blinking as I tore my gaze away from the GI hottie. Fuck, she was a dream. An especially unattainable dream.

"You will feel like death tomorrow but you can hook each other up with IV lines and a few banana bags," Acevedo added.

Hartshorn glanced up, frowning. His brow wrinkled as he studied Shannon and Acevedo. "Why the hell would we want to do that?"

"I can't explain it but I know it will help," Shannon said simply.

"It will," Acevedo agreed.

"It's a good spot to feel all of your misery and then leave it behind," Shannon said.

"I don't understand this at all," I said to Hartshorn. He shrugged.

"Before you take your misery to the bar," Andy called from the kitchen, "take some of these leftovers with you."

She was busying piling food into glass containers and then

packing them into grocery totes. "No," I said, holding up my hands. "Thank you, but no."

"It's no trouble," she continued as she filled a plastic bag with cookies. There was a big ass diamond on her ring finger now and it shouted 'unavailable' every time it hit the light.

"I really can't," I protested. I glanced at Hartshorn for help but he was waiting on bated breath for his goody bag.

Patrick secured the lid on one of the containers and speared me with a sharp look. "For reasons I cannot begin to comprehend, my fiancée wants to send you home with food. You're going to take it, you're going to be pleasant about it, and you're damn well going to enjoy it."

He thrust the tote in my direction and I closed my hands around the handle. "Yes, of course," I said. "Thank you."

Hartshorn and I headed toward the door, stopping for an endless series of goodbyes along the way. Once we were in the hall, he asked, "It wouldn't hurt to stop for one drink, right?"

"As long as we don't have to talk about feelings or shit like that," I said, "then no, it wouldn't hurt a damn thing."

He jerked a shoulder up. "One drink."

"One drink," I agreed.

I didn't remember much after that point, but I knew we shared many more than one drink.

Eleven

RILEY

"WHAT IS WRONG WITH YOU TONIGHT?" Alex asked when we rounded the landing after leaving Andy and Patrick's apartment.

"Nothing is wrong with me," I said, sliding my arm around her waist. "But that douche salad has a few misconceptions I'd like to correct."

"Who are you talking about?" she asked, throwing her hands up.

"Stremmel," I cried. "Obviously."

We reached the next landing and she shook her head. "You're insane."

"And you are really good at ignoring all the men who leer at you."

"No one leers at me except you," she chided.

"Stremmel leers," I said hotly. The blast of cold winter air as we hit the sidewalk did nothing to cool me down. "He's a dirty old leerer."

"Oh my god," she whispered, stomping ahead of me. "He's just trying to figure us all out."

I jogged to catch up to Alex. She was a short stack but she was quick on her feet. "He wants to figure out how to get you into bed."

"We have to agree to disagree on that point," she said. "No —wait. We're going to agree that it doesn't fucking matter because even if he's hitting on me, I'm not hitting back." She speared me with a fierce look. "I can resist manly charms, you know."

We were silent for several long minutes while we walked back to her apartment. "I know all that," I said as we turned the corner onto Cambridge Street. "Doesn't mean I have to like it and it doesn't mean I shouldn't want to feed him his tongue."

"Now that's some manly charm," she snapped.

We trudged up the stairs to her apartment without another word. It felt wrong. This wasn't the way we rolled. We didn't take anything too seriously, and when it did get heavy, we redirected it into something easy. Song lyrics and movie quotes. Tacos and beer. Rough sex and dirty photos. *That* was how we rolled.

We didn't do jealousy and we weren't that couple who yelled at each other on the sidewalk, and I wanted to keep it that way.

"Hey," I said as she slid her key into the lock. "Come here, Honeybee."

I pressed my lips to the sliver of skin visible between her scarf and hat, right behind her ear. My fingers fumbled with the front of her coat to find the zipper. It came down with a harsh whisper and her breath caught in her throat. As much as I wanted to, I didn't paw at her. I let my hands settle on her waist and held tight.

"I have something for you," I said.

"It better not be your dick in a box," she said with a laugh.

"That invites paper cuts and other injuries which I'd rather not suffer," I replied. I pushed the door open and helped her out of her coat. She set her phone and pager on the kitchen counter. She wasn't on call but that guaranteed a whole lot of nothing. "My something, it's for you, in accordance with our agreement."

"The agreement," she repeated, almost to herself. "Okay. Good. I have something for you, too." She pointed at me. "But you need to stay here for a minute."

She vanished into the bedroom, and the filthy part of my brain—that was, the majority of it—had visions of sugar tits dancing in my head. Those were homemade.

Minutes ticked by without a naked Honeybee emerging, and I decided I needed to stop standing in the middle of the room like a twat. I kicked my shoes off, turned the lights down low, and dug my gift out from its hiding place in my messenger bag.

Then she emerged…fully clothed.

"You go first," we said in unison, and then laughed.

"Ladies first," I said, the small package concealed behind my back.

"The lady wants you to go first," she said, smiling.

With a heavy sigh, I held out my gift. "Okay. I-I-I-I hope you don't hate it."

"I won't hate it," she said, studying the package.

It was wrapped in butcher paper and tied with twine, and I'd never doubted a piece of work so much in my life.

I should've gone with the guys to find the right combination of jewels and silk. Shannon was off her damn rocker. Alex and I had strict rules about where and how we stored our photos, and none of those included line sketches.

Fuck. Just...fuck. Christmas number one, up in flames. Down in shambles. Fucked right over.

This could only be worse if I actually started a fire.

She turned the package over, her brows knit together and her lips folded in concentration, and starting a fire sounded like a damn good idea right now.

Her finger slipped under the twine and I darted across the room, snatching it from her hands without considering my next move.

"I—uh—no," I stammered, holding the gift over my head. Alex couldn't reach it up there, and in this moment, a game of keep-away was the best, most mature solution available.

She crossed her arms and dropped onto the sofa as if I ripped presents out of her hands every day and this was the pinnacle of normal behavior. "What are you doing?" she asked.

"I don't know," I admitted. "I'm a li-li-li-li-little nervous."

"Why? Did you weld a set of nipple clamps?"

"No, I don't know anything about metallurgy, and I wasn't going to call up my college friends for a chat involving the specifications of your nippular regions, Alexandra."

"It sounds like you've given it real thought," she replied.

I scrubbed a hand down my face. The other hand was still in the goddamn air. "No," I said from behind my fingers. "I didn't consider welding nipple clamps. For fuck's sake."

"Can we open them together?" she asked. "If it helps, I'm just as nervous as you are."

I peeked at her through my fingers. "You don't look nervous. I look nervous. Real fuckin' nervous. You look like you're watching a rerun of *Friends*."

"It's a skill perfected over years of internship and residency," she replied. "No one trusts an anxious surgeon." She patted the cushion beside her. "Don't let me sit here all by myself."

I went. I didn't want to stand there, my hand suspended over my head like a moron, when I could scoop Alex up and deposit her in my lap. She held out a tiny box and I surrendered her gift.

"Together," she repeated, a note of warning in her voice.

"No shenanies," I promised.

I watched over her shoulder as she peeled back the paper and found the framed drawing. I wasn't opening my gift—it could wait an ever-loving second—but listened to her hums and breaths as she studied my portrait of her.

"Riley."

I didn't know how to interpret that tone. I was starting to think about protecting my testicles. "Mmhmm?"

"Riley," Alex repeated, her fingers flying to her lips. "You did this?" Like a kid caught red-handed, I nodded. "Is this—" She hummed, her fingers still on her lips. "Is this what you see? When you look at me?"

"Yes," I said. "Why? Do you hate it? I'll destroy it right now if you hate. Burn every last inch of it."

"I don't hate it at all." Her hand ghosted over the portrait, her index finger tracing the faint lines of the honeycomb I'd sketched into the background. "I look, uh—"

"Amazing," I whispered against her neck. "Luscious. Filthy. Perfect. All mine."

"You did this. I can't believe you made this for me," she said through a watery laugh. "You made this and I look like—like—beautiful, and I can't believe it. Jesus. My gift sucks."

"Unless it's a blowjob, I doubt that."

Alex laughed and pressed the frame to her chest. "You were supposed to open yours," she chided, her tone too gentle to feel like censure. "Together. At the same time. You and me."

"Sorry," I mumbled, yanking the ribbon from around the

box. "You come first, me second." I pried open the box, surprised she didn't grab the joke I'd teed up, and found a key inside. "It's a key."

"It is a key," Alex said with a stiff laugh. "It's a key to my apartment." She shrugged and stared at the frame again. "I thought maybe you'd want to stay here sometimes."

"I do stay here sometimes," I said, kissing her jaw. "As often as you let me."

"I thought, maybe," she continued, "if you had a key, you wouldn't have to wait for me to finish up at the hospital. You could just come here, and—and maybe you could stay here. As much as you want. Or, I don't know, all the time."

"All the time?" I repeated. "Like, officially?"

"My parents have been telling people we're engaged for the past month and a half," she said. "How much more official do you need?"

"That's a good point," I said, nodding. I did not regret announcing my intentions to Alex's parents last month. I did regret putting her in the murky position of fielding congratulatory messages and engagement gifts from her parents' friends back in Nevada. And because I created my own chaos, I'd told her I was going to marry her but hadn't actually proposed. Every day shambles right here. "It would be strange if I didn't live here."

"That's what I'm screaming about," she said.

I took the portrait and the key, and set them both on the coffee table. "I mean, we're basically married."

"Basically," she replied.

I blinked at her as the moment pulsed between us.

Am I supposed to do this now? Get down on one knee and ask her to have me, body, soul, and shambles?

There was a voice in the far back of my mind suggesting

that I move "basically" to "actually." I went right on blinking like a damn owl.

"Hey, Riley?"

I don't even have a ring.

"Yeah?" I replied, choking on air in the process.

I can't do this without a ring.

"Thank you for my drawing," she said, her cheeks heating as she spoke. "It feels like you put everything into it."

Even if I had a ring, I didn't know what I was supposed to say.

"I did," I admitted.

I don't know what to say or how to say it, and I don't have a ring. I am an idiot.

"I love it, and I love you," she said.

Is this it? Is this my opening?

"I've been stressing about this gift all week long," Alex continued. "I'm so relieved that you didn't freak out and tell me it's too soon to talk about living together—"

"Basically married, remember?"

Just fucking do it. Do it now, fix the mistakes later.

"Right," she said, laughing. "Since we've sorted that out, I want holiday movies, those cookies from the party, and my bed."

I ran my hand down her back and palmed her ass while I kissed her neck. "Are you kicking me out, Honeybee?"

"No, no," she said. "You're coming to bed with me."

This isn't our opening.

But also, it is.

"I'm going to marry you someday." I stood, Alex still cradled in my arms, and headed toward the bedroom. "Tonight, I'm gonna strip you naked and paint some holly leaves on your tits. I haven't decided where I'm drawing the mistletoe yet. I might experiment with that one. Sound good?"

"Perfect," she replied.

Twelve

THE COMMODORE

THE BABY WAS ASLEEP. The gifts were tucked under the tree and the stockings filled. Will and Shannon were home from the party and settling down for the night. Not a creature was stirring…except my wife.

"I just don't know why she hasn't told us," Judy said, slapping the comforter. She'd uttered some iteration of that statement at least ten times per day for the past thirty days.

"Haven't a clue," I said, closing my book but keeping my finger tucked between the pages. I didn't dare mention that she'd been hounding Lauren for a grandbaby since before her wedding day or that I sensed our youngest child was paying my wife back for the haranguing.

"It's obvious, isn't it?" Judy asked. "She must be almost three months along and she hasn't said a thing. I just don't understand it."

I glanced at the ceiling, sending up a prayer for patience. Even after thirty-nine years of marriage, plus five years of courting, Judy still tested every shred of my patience.

"She'll tell us in her time," I said. "Lolo has a plan for every-thing. I'm sure she has a plan for this."

"You say that about Wesley," she replied with an edge in her voice that told me I was skating on thin ice. "Look where that's led us."

"Wesley is private," I said. "It's his nature. He's always kept to himself, always taken his time to share things with us. When he was four, he went two days with a broken finger before mentioning it."

She huffed out a sigh that indicated she didn't care for my example. "I wasn't happy about that either."

"Will is a leader, Lolo is a planner, and Wesley is a vault. That's why he's so valuable to the clandestine services."

Judy shot out of bed to pace the length of the room. "Has it occurred to you that all of our children keep secrets from us? That they don't feel comfortable talking to us about the issues in their lives?"

"They haven't been children for ten or fifteen years, Judith Jane."

That earned me a sharp glare before she returned to wearing the rugs thin. I should've known better than to suggest our babies were all grown up or imply she was a heartbeat over twenty-eight.

"They don't keep secrets," I said, patting the empty spot beside me. She ignored the hint. "They work through chal-lenges independently and come to us once they've reached decisions or require counsel. They're smart and capable, and I am proud of their independence. We did well with them. *You* did well."

"If it's such a wonderful thing, then why does it bother me so much?"

She propped her hands on her red satin pajamas. I couldn't imagine the menswear style was meant to be alluring, but I had to drag my eyes away from the curve of her full hips in order to form a single thought.

"Up here, Bill." Judy snapped her fingers and pointed to her face. That coquettish smile. It was the death of me. From the first moment I spotted her after the Thanksgiving weekend University of Texas at Austin–Texas A&M game, that smile knocked me right over.

I'd found her on the front lawn of my fraternity house with a group of her girlfriends. It was hot as hell that day. November—even in Texas—had no business running that warm and it forced everyone outside late into the evening.

She wore a long floral dress, the off-the-shoulder kind without straps or sleeves. The twenty-something version of me believed—hoped—it would fall at any moment. Her blonde hair was knife-straight and brushed her waist, and she had a dandelion tucked over her ear. She was a little sprite of a lady, short and generously curved, and she shot down every man who dared walk her way. She drank Heineken from the bottle and belted out a laugh when I asked if she'd take a walk with me.

She laughed, but then she said yes.

I fell for her that night. Fell hard and fast, and all these years later, I hadn't stopped falling.

Back then, Judy had other things on her mind. She had big goals and bigger plans, and no time for boyfriends. Her brother's number came up in the draft, and she was determined to do her part, too. She was studying nursing, and intended to take her training to the armed services immediately after graduation. As far as she was concerned, her personal politics on

Vietnam mattered less than the fact she was capable of lending a hand to those in need. By that logic, she couldn't get overseas quick enough.

I hated everything about that, and she didn't give a good shit.

That was my last year at Austin. I was due in Virginia for the Navy's Special Forces training after accepting my diploma. I asked her to come with me, and then I begged. She had no interest in being a wife or setting up a home, not when she had another year of coursework to complete and then troops to aid, and there was no two ways about it.

I fought her on it, but that was as futile as begging her to marry me. Judy was a steamroller, and nothing was standing in her way. Not even me. As much as it drove me batty, I loved her conviction. The sense of purpose that went straight down to her marrow. It was that purpose that sent me to Virginia with the belief I'd get my ring on her finger someday.

It took nearly four years and the Fall of Saigon, but I succeeded.

Austin was in a different conference now, and they didn't play A&M over Thanksgiving weekend anymore. It was a shame. It was a hearty rivalry. I hated how the best things changed and nothing stayed the same anymore.

"Give her time," I said, my words rougher than intended. "Lolo will tell us soon enough."

Judy stared at me, her eyes flaring and lips twisting in frustration. Then she reached for a pillow and chucked it at my head. "You're getting on my last nerve. My very last nerve. I have a mind to make you sleep with the dogs."

She went for another pillow but I caught her wrist and flipped her onto the bed. My knees bracketed her hips and she was breathing heavy from the skirmish. "I'm still faster than you are, little bit."

She laughed, and the ripple of her body beneath mine was enough to get my motor running.

"Oh, please," she said, waving me off. "You only catch me because I let you."

"All these years," I said, thumbing open the buttons running down her shirt. "Have you been letting me win all along?"

She nodded, saying, "Of course not."

I freed the final button and pushed the silky fabric away. There was nothing like the sight of her.

"What's that face?" she asked, bringing her hand to my jaw.

"I still can't believe it," I murmured, my knuckles sliding up her belly. There was nothing softer than her skin. Nothing in the known world.

"Believe what?" she asked. "That I know all of your defensive maneuvers?"

"That you're mine," I said.

She cast her eyes down, a shy smile on her lips, and said, "Believe it, buddy. Can't get rid of me now."

I yanked my shirt over my head. "Your mission, should you choose to accept it, is to remain absolutely silent. Waking the baby or the kids will immediately terminate the mission. No joy for this hop. Understood?"

She made a sour face and shook her head as she yanked my pajama pants down. "I don't want to play *Mission: Impossible* tonight."

I stripped off her pants, and then mine, and returned to straddling her hips. My shaft was full and throbbing on her belly, but I wasn't moving until we finalized the rules of engagement. Silence was the target here. I was battle tested but

I couldn't withstand the torture of discussing my sex life with my son again.

"What's your pleasure, little bit?" I asked.

She rocked her head from side to side, humming as she considered this. "Let's play spy games."

"You can call me Bond. James Bond."

"Pussy Galore," she replied.

I worked hard at keeping my composure when my spunky little sorority girl made a point of dragging the word *pussy* out. Truth be told, it wasn't always this way. It wasn't always fun or easy, and we didn't always know how to play the way we wanted. Needed. But getting the kids out of the house helped, and the unending vacation of retired life helped, too.

"You best be quiet, Pussy," I said.

"And if I'm not?"

"If you can't stay quiet," I started, running my palm along her thigh, "there will be consequences. We can't risk the arms dealers finding out our location. If they hear us, they'll know. It will risk the entire operation."

Judy quirked up an eyebrow. "Don't you think they have an idea where we are, Mr. Bond?"

I reached for the small bottle of lube in the bedside table and poured some into my palm. "They might have a clue to our coordinates, but we can't tip them off." I slapped the side of her thigh. "They'll bring the hammer down on this operation."

"I prefer your hammer," she said with a wink.

"I know you do, Pussy," I said, running my slicked-up hand over my length. "I know you do." I squeezed her leg, nudging her. "On your belly. Face down. Bite the pillow if you have to because we need to keep this action off the radar."

She shifted, asking, "Is that why you pulled the bed away from the wall?"

I cracked my hand over her ass when it came into view. "Yes," I replied. There was no helping it. Every time I saw that round backside bare, I wanted to spank it.

"Good thinking, Mr. Bond," she replied with a giggle.

I PULLED up to the curb in front of Patrick's building, and glanced back at Lauren in the rearview mirror. "How are you doing, Miss Honey?"

"Wonderful," she said, her attention on her phone. "I could get used to this."

"I can't. I've reached for you five times in the past ten minutes. I'm experiencing wife withdrawals."

"Andy says they'll be down in a second." She held up her phone as proof. "I know this isn't your favorite seating arrangement but Patrick bitches and moans if he has to sit in the back seat and I didn't want to play musical chairs when we got here."

"I know. It's not a big deal. I'm just used to having you next to me." I shifted to face her. "I'm going to ask one last time."

"The answer is still no," she replied, layering her hands over her abdomen. She was wearing a loose dress that concealed the slight roundness in her belly. "Let my mother and everyone else dote on Shannon. I don't want to take anything away from her."

"I'm certain Shannon won't feel neglected." Part of me wanted to make a big announcement. The other part liked keeping my wife content. "She might welcome the reprieve. When I talked to her last night, she seemed to suggest she needed a break from everyone."

"Maybe," she said, unconvinced. "But I want to cross that twelve-week threshold first."

"Then that's what we'll do," I said. We were crossing that threshold in two days but I didn't get the impression Lauren was interested in hearing my logic on the matter.

She frowned, and touched her fingertips to her lips. "My mother's head will explode when we tell her about the baby."

Lauren was right about that. I'd built ample guest quarters in the new house plans for a reason. "And your father will feed me to the sharks."

"He will not," she replied. "He'll glare at you for several minutes and then he'll be thrilled. No shark bait."

"Can we tell them about the house?" I asked, hopeful. We had a verbal agreement with the seller, and I had a fuck-ton of work ahead of me. I was thinking about juggling my upcoming projects to add some breathing room to my sched-ule. Maybe poaching one of Patrick's assistants. The next few months were going to be hectic.

"I'm not—" The doors opened and Patrick and Andy piled in, their arms loaded with gifts. "I'm not sure," Lauren said over their greetings.

"You look adorable," Andy said, running her fingertips down the sleeve of Lauren's cranberry red dress. "Is this new?"

"It is," Lauren said, catching my eye in the mirror. "I was doing some last minute shopping after school, and it called to me."

"Hmmm." Andy nodded as she gave the dress careful

inspection. "It looks really comfortable," she said. "It's cute. This is a good style for you."

"Thank you," Lauren said with a sunny smile. "It *is* comfortable."

"Where's it from?" Andy asked.

"It's, uh," she started, "I'm blanking on the name."

I glanced over my shoulder, locking eyes with Lauren. "Last chance," I mouthed to her, knowing the garment was a find from a trendy maternity shop. She shook her head.

"A little place off Newbury," she replied. "I can't remember the name but I'll point it out the next time we're in that neighborhood."

"You should've told me you were going out," Andy said. "You could've met up with me and Tiel. We had a very special visit to one your favorite boutiques. The dressing rooms are sensational."

"Andy," Patrick growled.

Choking down a laugh, I gestured to the foil-wrapped dish on Andy's lap. "What do you have there?"

"Lasagna," she said. "Shannon texted me at four o'clock this morning because she was awake and wandering around the house. Apparently she was *very* hungry and wanted—"

"For fuck's sake, people. If we wanted to sit at the curb and converse for twenty minutes, we would've caught a ride with Sam," Patrick said.

"Sam doesn't have room for us," Andy said. "He has the baby and Ellie. Remember?"

"I'm not interested in those details," Patrick replied. "But if this is the pace we're going, I could walk to Shannon's house faster."

Andy rolled her eyes while Lauren rocked in silent laughter. "Then you should do that, Patrick. Get out and jog alongside the car."

I settled into my seat and put the car in gear. "Doesn't get any merrier than this."

***

"WHITE OR RED, LAUREN?" Riley asked, a bottle in each hand as we settled into Shannon's dining room.

"You know, I think I'll stick with water," she replied.

Riley chuckled, shaking his head. "Yeah, that's funny but really," he said. "White or red?"

She shrugged as if she declined wine every day. "I think I'll skip the wine for now. I'll have some later."

"None of my special holiday creations last night, no wine with dinner," Riley said. "What's happening to you? Are you dying? Are you doing some fucked-up cleanse where you stop eating and drinking the best things in life?" He clutched the bottles to his chest. "Holy Hannah, are you pregnant?"

"Finally!" Judy shrieked and pressed her hands to her chest. "Is it true, Lolo?"

Abby and Dave took this as an invitation to join the shrieking from their side-by-side high chairs, and it dawned on me that our child would be joining them soon enough.

"I knew it," Tiel said with a fist pump. "You little secret-keeper."

"What are you talking about?" Lauren cried. "You guys are crazy. Stop it. I skip drinks all the time."

Shannon stared at her from the far end of the table. "Never once," she said, holding up a finger. "You have never once declined a drink. Don't you remember the time we went out for dinner and instead of leaving a half-finished cocktail, you emptied Abby's sippy cup and dumped your drink in there?"

"I don't see the issue with that," Lauren said.

"Neither do I. It's conservation," Andy added. "The best thing about having kids is the sippy-cup-cocktail routine."

"There might be a few other things," Nick said.

"Hey, Matt," Sam called. "You're gripping that fork damn hard. This might be a good time to think about putting it down, taking a breath, blinking."

Riley reached over and relieved me of the utensil. "I'm gonna look after this for you."

"I know pregnant boobs," Tiel said with a pointed look at Lauren's cleavage. "Pregnant boobs don't lie."

When I recovered from the quick snap of shock from Riley beating us to this announcement, I glanced over at Lauren. She had a tight smile plastered on her face and her hand flattened on her abdomen.

"This wasn't the plan," she whispered.

"It's never your plan, Sweetness."

Her shoulders shook with laughter. "You're always rearranging my plans."

"Hardly." I took her hand in mine and glanced up at our family. "Yes, we are having a baby."

"It is about time," Judy said. "I can't wait. Cannot wait! I'm just thrilled. Let's get some champagne."

"Yeah, you do that," Lauren said. "I'm having the baby but the rest of you should definitely celebrate with alcoholic beverages while I watch. That makes perfect sense."

"Is anyone else pregnant? Are there any other announcements?" Shannon asked, one hand on her lower back, the other waving at the people seated around her table. "Let's get it all out now. I can't do multiple rounds of this. We can discuss and eat at the same time."

The collective gaze shifted from Riley and Alex to Patrick and Andy and then Nick and Erin.

"Don't look at us," Erin said. "We already earned our big holiday dinner announcement badge last year. We're good on that front."

"Yeah, I think we're maxed out on announcements. The secret marriage was plenty," Nick said. "We're good."

"My pants are zipped," Riley said. "That's the best I have for you today."

"Let's get back to Matt and Lauren," Andy said. "When is this baby arriving?"

"Early July," Lauren said. "My plan is to make it through the school year."

"There you go again with the plans," I murmured.

"This is the best news I've heard all day," Judy said. "Isn't this the best, Bill? We need some champagne."

The Commodore's gaze settled on me for a long, painful moment where it was obvious he was fighting off the knowledge that I'd defiled his daughter. "It's wonderful news," he said. "I'll rustle up the bubbly, Judy, don't you worry."

"You get the champagne," Shannon said as she pushed to her feet. "This kid is killing me. I need to walk around. I'll grab some sparkling water so Lauren doesn't feel left out."

My father-in-law followed Shannon into the kitchen but not before tossing a sharp glimpse at me over his shoulder. I didn't think anyone else noticed as they were too busy lavishing my wife with well wishes but I saw it.

"Your dad wants to kill me," I whispered to Lauren.

"No, he doesn't," she replied. "He's stoic, that's all."

I was about to disagree with her but then glass shattered in the kitchen. Shannon cried out and Will was on his feet, sprinting into the next room with all of us in tow. We found her hunched over with the Commodore at her side, a broken bottle at her feet.

"What the hell happened here?" Will asked.

Andy picked her way through the crush of people and bent to collect the chunks of broken glass. "Let's handle this first," she said. "No one move. Keep the dogs and kids in the other room. We'll get everything cleaned up." She spared a look at Shannon. "Are you doing all right, mama?"

"My water broke," Shannon said through a groan.

Beside me, Alex and Nick exchanged a glance. "This one is all you," she whispered to him. "I don't know the first thing about childbirth."

"Bullshit," Nick mouthed. "That's really fuckin' false, Alex."

"What?" Will roared. "What are you talking about, Shannon? We have three more weeks and—"

"And this kid doesn't give a fuck," Shannon replied. "I started having contractions last night—"

"What do you mean you've been having contractions since last night? You didn't think to mention that highly critical news to me?" Will asked.

On my other side, Lauren rested her head on my shoulder. "One of these years, we'll have a low-key holiday," she murmured.

"When did this start?" Will asked. "While we were in the city or after—"

"After," Shannon yelled. "After we came home and had that long *conversation*." She shot a fierce, pointed glare in his direction. "I didn't want to alert you because you know that I usually have light contractions after vigorous conversations."

Behind me, Riley asked, "Does anyone else think *conversation* might be code for something?"

"I don't think we're meant to ask questions right now," Lauren said to him.

"That was eighteen hours ago," Will said.

"They slowed down," Shannon said. "But then they sped up."

"I haven't delivered a baby since my first year of residency," Alex whispered. "You take this, Acevedo. Call me when there's a peptic ulcer or some diverticulitis. Hell, I'll treat stomach viruses and acid reflux before I'll deliver a baby."

"Goddamn it, Shannon," Will said, groaning.

"You two aren't making me feel any better about this situation," I said to Nick and Alex. "Shouldn't you do something?"

Nick clapped me on the back. "I'm on it, Walsh. Don't worry."

Shannon cried out and wrapped both hands around Will's arm. He ran his free hand down her back, whispering something I couldn't hear. Nick stepped away from us and edged around Andy as she cleaned up the broken bottle. He moved to Shannon's side, and rested one hand on her back and one on her belly.

"That one was for real," she said, her cheeks flushed and breath coming fast.

"Yes, it was." Nick glanced at his watch. "We should go. I don't want you to progress much farther."

Andy dropped the shards into a paper bag, and in that moment, the clink and crunch of glass was the only sound in the kitchen. Then, everyone talked at once while I watched in stunned silence.

Judy: We need to get you out of those wet clothes, sweetheart.

Lauren: Where's the hospital bag? Nevermind, I'll find it myself.

Will: Do you really think we have time for a wardrobe change, Judy?

Patrick: What is happening right now?

Shannon: I need the blanket. The little one with the purple elephants.

The Commodore: I'll pull the car around.

Erin: I'll find the elephants.

Alex: I'll give your doctor a call.

Tiel: I'll grab some towels. You can never have too many towels after your water breaks.

Patrick: No, really. What's happening?

Sam: Is anyone getting a mop? Because…you know… someone should do that.

Ellie: I'm taking Abby and Dave into the playroom. We're gonna learn some tunes and pretend everyone isn't screaming.

Will: I have to call Shaw. Where's my phone?

Nick: Would someone grab my medical kit out of the car?

Patrick: Someone tell me what's going on.

Shannon: It's in your motherfucking hand, Will.

Riley: Should we boil some water? Isn't that what you're supposed to do?

Erin: Purple elephants!

Judy: I have a change of clothes!

Alex: She doesn't need a cup of tea, babe.

Sam: I don't think we're paying enough attention to the mop situation.

Patrick: So, it's happening right now? *Now* now?

Riley: I'm pretty sure we're supposed to boil water.

Lauren: Where do you think babies comes from, Patrick?

Erin: Let me take your bracelets and necklaces, Shannon.

I'll put them upstairs. You don't need them getting in your way.

Nick: The only reason to boil water is to give the father a chore when he's in the way.

Will: We're going right now.

Sam: Okay, so we're ignoring the floors?

The Commodore: Got the kit, Doc.

Shannon: I'm not leaving yet. I'm not ready.

Will: What, you'd like to wait another eighteen hours?

Shannon: I want to take a shower and spend some time with Abby and—

Nick: This baby has a different plan, Shannon.

Riley: I'll boil the water. Just in case.

Sam: Fuck it. I'm getting the bleach.

Tiel: We'll stay with Abby tonight. Don't worry about a thing.

Will: Peanut. *Now*.

Erin: You've got this. Go. We'll see you soon.

The chaos migrated from the kitchen to the foyer and then into Will's SUV while I stood by, struck by the panic of it all. I wasn't ready for this.

"This is going to be us," Lauren whispered.

I tugged her closer to me. This moment felt too bright, too fast, and I didn't know how to respond. "Hopefully we won't follow this exact playbook." My stomach churned at the thought.

"We'll see," she said with a laugh.

"No, Miss Honey," I replied. "You're not allowed to go into labor without telling me."

"You're going to be fine," Lauren said, squeezing my hand. "*We* are going to be just fine."

We stood at the door, watching as the SUV's tail lights faded from sight.

"What's the etiquette here? Can we finish eating?" Riley asked, looking at each of us. "I think Shannon would want us to enjoy this meal. It's not like we can do anything right now. She's the one with the vagina and baby and all of those things. We can't help with the birthing of the child. We can support her by enjoying this delicious dinner, and once it's finished, we can go to the hospital and meet Tinkerbelle."

Andy gasped. "It's a girl? You knew? When did Shannon tell you?"

Riley waved his arms at her. "Out of everything I just said, that's what you heard?"

"I vote that we eat," Patrick said, his hand raised.

Riley pointed at Patrick. "Optimus is the boss. We have to do what he says."

"My god, don't repeat that," Sam muttered. "He might start to believe it."

"COORDINATES?" the Commodore asked as he pulled out of the driveway.

"Just get on the damn highway, Dad," Will snapped, his phone pressed to his ear. "Shaw, unless you're handling an international incident, I expect a call back in the next minute. And if you are handling an incident, call me back and then call Kaisall."

"Boston," Shannon yelled. "Head for the city. I'll give you directions to the women's hospital from there."

She was sandwiched between Judy and me in the back seat, and I had both hands on her belly. I was counting the seconds —we were on a seconds basis here—between spasms but I wasn't convinced I had the timing right. It couldn't be right. She couldn't be progressing this fast. But seconds later, I felt her muscles tighten again.

"We don't have time," I said.

"We're going to make time." Her eyes flashed with panic. "You don't get to tell me there's no time," she continued, waving her hands to the side, tears filling her eyes.

"There are thresholds to this, Shannon," I said. "This baby is coming very quickly, and I can't promise we have the time to get you to Brigham. It's on the far side of the Back Bay. That's another half hour that I don't believe we have, and we'd drive right past Mass General on the way. Let me call Hartshorn, and he'll page everyone in OB. We'll take great care of you."

"But I don't want that," Shannon wailed, tears spilling over. "I want *my* hospital and *my* doctor and *my* plan, and this isn't that."

"And I don't want you delivering your baby in the back seat of this car," I said.

Will shifted in his seat, the phone still at his ear, and stared at Shannon. "Peanut," he said, desperation heavy in his tone. "Please. I know it's not what you want, and hell, it's not what I want either, but listen to Nick right now."

"Look at me, sweetheart." Judy tucked Shannon's hair over her ears. "We're going to do this, and it's going to be all right. Just hold my hand."

We were flying down the highway, driving faster than seemed safe or possible with snow falling in heavy sheets. "You'll have to push soon," I said. "You don't want to do that here."

"Okay," Shannon said, sniffling. "But I want to state, one more time, that this is not what I wanted."

"And I want to state that it won't happen again," Will replied.

"Again?" Shannon yelled. "You think we're doing this again? The first chance I get, I'm cutting off your balls and making lawn ornaments with them."

"Oh really?" Will replied. "First chance I get, I'm going to remind you that I was right. I told you that you were doing too much, I told you to sit the fuck down, and I told you to stop pushing yourself. If you did what you were told, we wouldn't be in this position."

"If you want to talk to me about *this position*, you can do it while you suck my dick," she said.

"No, Shannon, I can't fucking do that right now because I need to reroute the security team I had in place at the other hospital," he said. "Forgive me, but I'll have to catch your dick later."

"Why the fuck do you have a security team in place?" she asked. "Goddamn it, Commando. There are too many issues to list right now."

"Why *wouldn't* I have a team?" he replied.

"I know this is your normal, but it would be great if y'all could scream at each other a little less," I said. I caught Shannon's eye as I pressed my fingers to the pulse point in her wrist. "We don't need your heart rate and blood pressure going through the roof."

"My blood pressure would be fine if it weren't for the mansplainer in the front seat," she said.

"Your blood pressure would be fine if you listened to reason from time to fucking time," Will replied.

The Commodore whistled and pointed at Will. "This is one of the instances in life where your opinions are less useful than rubber dog shit, and I've never found a use for rubber dog shit," he said. "Shut it, or I'll leave you on the side of the road. Don't forget that I outrank you."

"As if I could forget," Will muttered.

"Let's talk about names," Judy suggested as she massaged Shannon's abdomen. "Which ones are on your list, sweetheart?"

"Stop trying to find out the sex, Judy," Will said, furiously stabbing at his phone as he spoke. He pressed the device to his ear, still fuming. "Shaw, I mean it when I say I'll fly to Virginia and beat the snot out of you tonight if you don't call me back immediately."

"Leave Shaw out of this," Shannon said. "We do not need a military unit on standby. We didn't have one with Abby."

"If that's what you want to believe, let yourself believe it," he murmured.

"Are you fucking kidding me? Would it kill you to run any of this shit by me before—" Shannon shrieked as another contraction hit. "I fucking hate you right now, Commando."

Will tossed his phone to the center console and shifted in his seat to take both of her hands in his. "Give it to me. Come on, Peanut, I have you."

I pulled my phone from my pocket and wedged it between my ear and shoulder while Judy and I rubbed Shannon's lower back through the worst of the spasms. The first and second calls went to voicemail, a sure sign that Hartshorn was in surgery. That was not the way I wanted this situation to pan out. I tried a few other numbers, but they all went to voicemail or the surgical answering service system. With a reluctant sigh, I called the only other doctor I knew to be working tonight.

"Doctor Stremmel," he answered.

"Hey," I replied, stretching the word out as I made peace with this decision. I had to remind myself that he was the top trauma surgeon on the West Coast, and we were lucky to have him and his piss-pleasant attitude. "It's Nick Acevedo."

"The wonders of caller ID notified me of this before I answered," he replied. "What can I do for you, Doctor Acevedo?"

"You're holding down the Emergency Department, right? How's the board tonight? Busy? What's going on?"

"Yes, empty, slow, and not much. In that order," he replied.

"I'm heading in with my sister-in-law, Shannon. She's thirty-seven weeks and in active labor with contractions about fifty seconds apart."

"The one from—from last night? The one that I—"

"Yes," I interrupted. "Who's the OB attending tonight?"

He groaned as if I'd punched him in the gut. "Zellers but she just scrubbed in with preterm twins," he said. "She has four residents. Two of them are handling unremarkable deliveries. Two of them can't tell an elbow from an asshole. I wouldn't let those two give me a flu shot."

"Do me a favor and don't page those two," I said. "Who else is on?"

"Me and Northcutt," Stremmel said, "but he's in the OR, setting a broken hip. Icy sidewalks are a real problem out here, huh?"

"You're right about that," I murmured.

"Ten minutes," the Commodore called.

I glanced up as the city skyline came into view. "Did you hear that?"

He murmured in agreement and I heard him ask someone nearby to prepare a room for delivery and call an obstetrics resident. "We'll be ready. I'll meet you outside," Stremmel said. "Hold up. Is her husband going to kill me?"

I studied Will for a second, his eyes trained on Shannon while she strangled the shit out of his hands. "It's anyone's guess but I'd suggest you proceed with an abundance of caution."

"Got it," he replied.

I ended the call and met Judy's gaze over Shannon's head. Her lips were folded in a tight line, and it was obvious that she knew we were running out of time.

"You're doing great, Shannon," I said.

"I don't need a gold star right now, Nick," she replied. "I'm having a baby on Christmas, my husband has a fully armed battalion at the hospital—"

"If Shaw ever answers his damn phone," Will muttered.

"—and I didn't get any pie," Shannon said. "I wanted some pie."

"I'll save you plenty of pie," the Commodore called. "We'll restart our late night diapers and desserts routine."

"I know how you are about pie," she replied. "I don't know that you have it in you to resist temptation."

He laughed as he merged onto Leverett Circle, weaving through traffic as if he was playing *Grand Theft Auto*. "For you, my dear, I can be good," he said. "I won't touch the cranberry apple or the chocolate cream."

We pulled into the ambulance bay, the tires screeching as we came to a stop. Stremmel waited on the curb, his hands shoved into the pockets of his lab coat and his shoulders hunched against the blowing snow.

Will burst from the vehicle and opened my door, shoving me out of the way as he reached for Shannon. "I'm sorry about everything I said, Peanut. I didn't mean any of it."

"Don't start lying to me now," she said, her arms around his neck and her face pressed to his chest.

He scooped her up and held her close, whispering into her hair as he marched ahead. Then he spotted Stremmel.

"Not this fucking guy," Will said with a groan.

"I'm probably the last person you want to see," Stremmel said as he steered Will toward the nurses and residents waiting inside the doors with a gurney

"Too right," Will replied.

"We don't have time to argue about it, Will," I said as the

automatic doors whooshed open. "I wouldn't have called Stremmel if I didn't trust him."

"That doesn't make me feel any better," Will grumbled. He set Shannon on the gurney, and we jogged toward an enclosed treatment room.

"It's worth noting that I've delivered hundreds of babies," I added. "I know what I'm doing. Between me and Stremmel, we've got this covered."

The team descended on Shannon, running intravenous lines and securing a fetal heart monitor while Judy coached her through another contraction.

"I'm having trouble believing that you and"—he pointed at Stremmel—"this fucking guy are our options right now. In this entire hospital, the best options are the guy who tried to pick up my wife last night and you?"

"Fully dilated," the resident announced. "Fully effaced."

"What did I do?" I asked, snapping on a pair of gloves.

"I don't know but I'm not happy about it," Will replied.

"I know you're having a dude standoff and it would be thoroughly entertaining on any other occasion," Shannon said. "But I need to push and if you don't shut up, I will castrate every last one of you and then carry your balls in a pretty little jar."

"You heard her," Stremmel said as a nurse helped him into a surgical gown. "This is Shannon's show. If you can't follow her rules, I'll have you removed." He turned to Shannon. "It's time to meet your baby."

I TORE off my surgical gown and dropped it in the soiled linens bin before heading toward the waiting room. Everyone was there, and they were fighting over desserts. A small table was covered with an assortment of goodies, and Andy was loading up paper plates to appease the grabby hands around her.

Erin, my little lovely, was picking at a brownie while Matt and Patrick carried on an animated conversation beside her. I watched for a minute, smiling when she sensed my gaze and glanced up. I beckoned her closer, needing a moment with her before sharing the good news with everyone.

She handed her plate to Patrick—who went on arguing with Matt while demolishing the brownie—and moved toward me. We ducked around the corner, out of sight. I wrapped my arms around her and pressed my lips to her forehead as she melted into me.

"Is she all right?" Erin asked.

"Mother and baby are doing well," I said. "I'm still a little rattled. There were a few minutes where I thought we'd meet her on the Tobin Bridge."

"How's Will? Did he survive the ordeal?" she asked around a laugh.

"It was touch-and-go with him," I replied, "especially when he realized Stremmel was handling the delivery. He's resting comfortably now and Stremmel is relatively unscathed."

Erin ran her hands up my flanks and over my shoulders, and I responded by backing her further into the corner. "Can I tell you a secret?" she whispered, glancing up at me with those green green green eyes.

I flattened my hands on the wall and ducked down to kiss her. She tasted like chocolate and secrets, and I ached for her. With my lips brushing the corner of her mouth, I whispered, "Always."

"I want to make some changes," she said, dipping her chin as she spoke.

My lips found hers again and I murmured, "Okay."

"I want to travel less frequently," she continued.

"Okay," I repeated. "I won't fight you on that."

"And I want a baby," she added.

Without conscious thought, I shifted closer, trapping her hips against mine. My heart was in my throat and it took a full minute to find words. "In theory?" I asked. "Or practice?"

"Practice," she replied, the word breaking into a moan as I rocked against her. "Not right now. Not tonight."

"If not tonight," I teased, "tomorrow?"

She squeezed my shoulders and I was half hard. "Maybe in the next year, or the year after."

"What about your field work?" I asked.

"I have an expedition on my schedule for October," she said, "but nothing after that. I've passed several studies onto research fellows."

"You'll go into withdrawal without field work," I said.

She turned her gaze to my shirt, shaking her head as she scowled at my buttons. "I would've agreed with that statement six months ago," she said. "But now? I'm not sure. I realized while I was in the Solomons that I've visited almost every corner of this planet. I've seen every extreme earth has to offer and—and I'm not sure I need continue seeking out those extremes. Not all the time. I have a lab and a data team now. I can devote more of my time writing and advocating for policy change. I want to give that a try."

"You've been thinking about this," I said. "You've worked it all out."

"Close to it." She shrugged. "I had to make sense of it for myself first. Before I met you, I never thought I was meant for marriage and kids. Never thought I could manage either. Never thought I wanted them. But now I know that I decide what I'm meant for, and I know you want us to start a family—"

I grabbed the waist of her jeans and flipped the button open with my thumb while she yelped. "Say the word and I'll put a baby in your right now, darlin'," I growled.

"You heard what I said about waiting a year or two, right?"

"I did," I replied, stroking the tender skin below her belly button.

"Are you worried that you won't remember the process?"

"Bite your tongue," I said. "No, Erin, I—" The words lodged in my throat. I always knew we'd find ourselves at this point. I knew we'd share a home, a name, a life. But that didn't make it any less remarkable when I realized we were already there. "I love you."

"I love you too," she replied.

"Care to visit an on-call room with me?" I asked. "You'll really love me after ten minutes in a windowless room."

"As much as I appreciate that offer, I want to meet my niece," she said, laughing.

I didn't share an ounce of her humor. I was estimating the number of steps to the closest on-call room.

"Stop growling at me," she said, swatting my arm. "I promise, this will work in your favor. Five minutes with that little munchkin and I'll be delirious with baby fever."

I kissed her hard, hard enough to leave her breathless. "I'm holding you to that," I said as I leaned back to adjust my cock. "Come on then. We have a baby to meet."

"ANNABELLE," I said as I arranged the toque on her head. "Annabelle Erin."

Will murmured in agreement and pressed his lips to the crown of my head. I was sure my hair was sweaty and gross, and I was also sure Will didn't care.

"Annabelle is just precious," Judy cooed from the other side of the room. She was digging through my bag for the muslin blanket I'd packed.

"You're amazing," Will whispered. He brought his hand to rest on Annabelle's back. "I can't even comprehend your strength, Peanut."

Judy appeared at my side and tucked some loose strands over my ear. "What do you need, sweetheart? What can I do for you?"

Tears filled my eyes when I realized Judy couldn't give me the one thing I needed. "I want my mom," I said through a sob.

"I know," she said.

"It's not fair," I said.

"Not at all," she replied through her own tears. "I'm so

sorry she's not here, sweetheart. She'd be proud of you, of the woman you've become. I know I'll never fill that void but I'm going to do the best I can for you."

"I couldn't do this without you," I said. "Thank you for being here. For everything."

"It is my pleasure, Shannon," she said, thumbing tears off my cheeks. "I'll always be here for you. You're one of mine, and that's never going to change."

I shook my head, too overcome with the adrenaline crash and rush of hormones to make words from my emotions. The tears spilled over and streaked down my cheeks. They poured out, out, out while Will whispered things I couldn't process but didn't think I'd ever forget.

Judy squeezed my hand and brought my head to her shoulder. "I know, sweetheart," she said. "I know."

I believed that. She knew, even though I couldn't put any of it into words. It didn't matter that Judy had only been in my life a few short years. She was the adult in the room when I needed one, the woman who answered every one of my crazy pregnancy questions and loved me like one of her own. She was the one who held me while I gave birth to my babies, who was the strength when I ran out of my own.

There was a quick knock at the door and Stremmel stepped in. "You have a small mob waiting outside," he said. "They're getting a little rowdy."

"Is Riley mixing drinks?" I asked. I was trying to laugh but only ended up crying harder.

Stremmel glanced over his shoulder and then back at us. "I don't know," he said, his impatience obvious. "I can send them in or send them home, but I'm not letting them hang out in my ER much longer."

I sniffled and asked, "Is my sister here?"

"Which one is that?" Stremmel asked.

Will sighed. "The other redhead," he said.

Judy kissed my temple and squeezed my hand again. "I'll go get her," she said. "We'll give the others a few minutes to simmer down, okay?"

"Can you check on Abby, too?" I asked. Goddamn these tears. They didn't stop. "I just want to make sure she's asleep and she's not too confused, and tell her we'll be home tomorrow—"

"No, Peanut," Will said. "That's not accurate."

"Are you sure?" Stremmel interrupted, swiping at his tablet. "Vaginal births are usually—"

"Don't say *vaginal* around my wife," Will snapped. "Just fuckin' don't. Thank you for delivering this perfect little girl and taking great care of my wife, but I haven't reconciled the fact you hit on her last night and then, you know—"

Stremmel cut him off with an irritable wave. "Yeah, all right," he murmured. "Anyway, I'd like you to stay at least twenty-four hours."

"I am going home whenever the fuck I'm ready to go home, and neither of you will bossy-penis me," I whisper-yelled over Annabelle's head. "I've had enough bossy-penis today, thank you."

Stremmel tucked his tablet under his arm, nodding. "Understood," he replied. He ducked his head and stared at his sneakers for a long beat. "Sorry about last night."

"Mmhmm," Will growled beside me.

"You're fine," I said. Still crying. "It was incredibly flattering." "My husband had quite a bit to say about it afterward. We had an extensive conversation."

I shot a smile in Will's direction, a quiet reminder of the

hour he spent between my legs while he made damn sure I knew how he felt about Stremmel's comments.

"For fuck's sake, Shannon," Will said.

"You did most of the talking," I said to Will, chuckling through my tears.

Judy cleared her throat. "Oh, my," she said. "I'll just go grab Erin and then I'll check on Miss Abigael. I'm sure she's doing well. I know Sam and Tiel are holding down the fort. She's probably tickled to have a sleepover with her cousin."

Stremmel glowered at his tablet. "Doctor Zellers will be taking over your case from here. We'll get you into a patient room, and she'll drop in as soon as she's available," he said. He checked the IV line on my hand and glanced down at Annabelle. "She's a cute kid."

"That's the only way we make them," I said.

He stared at Annabelle and I noticed the glimmers of a smile pulling at his lips. It was gone as quickly as it appeared. "I have patients to see," he said. "Press the call button if you need anything."

Stremmel left the room, and Will wrapped me and Annabelle up in his arms. He held me tight while tears continued rolling down my cheeks.

The last time I had a baby, I cried because my sister came home. I didn't understand why I was crying now—other than being buried under a landslide of hormones—or how to make it stop. I had every emotion hitting me at once.

Joy for my healthy baby girl.

Love for her, and Will and Abby.

Sadness that I was experiencing another milestone without my mother.

Fear that I wouldn't be able to manage two children, a job, a marriage, my family. That I wouldn't be good enough.

Regret that I hadn't spent more one-on-one time with Abby before her sister arrived.

Shock that I'd found the one man who didn't hesitate to argue with me while I gave birth to his child.

Hope that, despite my previous assertions, I'd have several more blonde babies with that man.

All of it surrounded me, and every time I sensed myself reaching the end, a new torrent knocked me sideways.

He leaned down and brushed his lips over mine, quick and sweet like a tiny promise. "I don't know how you do it," he said. "I don't know how you give all of yourself to everyone. Your brothers, your babies, me. You do it, and you ask nothing in return. None of us deserve you, Shannon."

"Is that why snipers and covert agents have the building surrounded?"

"It's one of the many reasons," he replied with a laugh. "I'll do whatever it takes to keep my girls safe. That's never going to change."

Another wave of emotion washed over me. It was a complicated mixture of rage and relief. As much as I pushed back on Will's caution and concern, I never doubted that he would guard my babies with his life. He'd do the same for me, too. And that was where the rage came in. My father betrayed me in a way I'd never reconcile. He stole parts of me I'd never reclaim. No one kept me safe, no one protected me.

"You're the best father." I was a bawling, blubbering mess, and Will knew it. He plucked Annabelle's hat from her head and mopped my tears with it. "I'm happy you didn't get that vasectomy because I want more babies."

"We're going to wait a little while before we get to work on our next baby. Months. Several months. Maybe a year," he said, tracing Annabelle's chubby cheeks. "You took years off my life today, Peanut. I don't want to panic like that ever again."

"Does that mean you'll be wearing a condom?" I asked.

He snickered. "Let's not get carried away here."

Judy returned with Erin in tow, and my sister wedged herself onto the gurney, bracketing me between her and my husband. Neither said anything for several minutes. They just held me and Annabelle, and slowly, slowly, I found my footing again.

"This time isn't my fault," Erin whispered while she stroked Annabelle's little fingers. "Must be your fault, Will."

He brushed the tears from my cheeks and kissed my forehead. "I'll take this one," he replied. "I'll take all of them."

ANDY'S HAND FOUND MINE, and she tugged me back, away from the wild crush surrounding Will and Shannon. And the red-faced creature on Shannon's chest. I didn't look too closely. It looked—the baby, she looked impossibly small. Abby, Dave, this one—they all seemed incomprehensibly tiny. Like those awkward internet videos of baby hedgehogs that were the size of a thumbnail.

I couldn't believe anything that small could be here. I didn't understand how anyone could care for such a delicate thing. I couldn't keep a sandwich intact long enough to eat it. I definitely couldn't handle a baby.

But also, I couldn't stop thinking about trading places with Will and Shannon. I saw Andy in that bed, her hair piled high and her cheeks glowing, and our baby nestled between her breasts.

Andy glanced over at me with a bright smile. "Precious, isn't she?" she said as I leaned closer to hear, nodding in agreement. I didn't have another response. This wasn't the time to mention I was simultaneously terrified that I'd accidentally manhandle our hypothetical future child and wondering when we could get to work on making that child. That, and it was too fucking loud in here for a conversation.

The room was ten miles past out of control and closing in on mayhem. I couldn't believe Will tolerated this ruckus. I wanted to get in the middle to manage this situation like one of my properties. Everyone needed a task. Something to do. Something to keep them busy because there was no reason for them to be hovering over the newborn.

"She's going to be a towhead, just like Abby," she continued.

I nodded again as I stared into her dark eyes. I could drown in those eyes, and I had, more times than I could recount. Andy was home to me. My quiet in a noisy world. My softness when everything was sharp edges and right angles.

"We should go," I said, my eyes dropping to her lips.

"Yeah," she replied, mirroring my gaze. "Let them settle in. We'll be seeing plenty of Annabelle soon."

We pushed through the hive of new baby excitement but not before several conversations with my siblings and Shannon's in-laws. They all wanted to discuss the series of events that brought us here tonight and the surprise arrival of the newest member of our tribe.

When we finally reached Shannon's side, she beckoned me closer and said, "You've been quiet."

I nodded—that was all I could fucking do tonight—and ran my finger over Annabelle's downy white-blonde hair. "A lot on my mind," I said.

"Me too," she said with a watery laugh. "You should get out of here. It might not look like it, but I have this situation under control. It helps that we have a handful of doctors in the family now."

"You always have it under control," I said. I leaned forward, folding her into an awkward one-armed hug while also holding myself away to keep from smothering the baby.

When I stepped back, Andy took my place. "You know this isn't a race, right?" she asked. "You don't have to show us all up by popping out five kids before most of us have one."

I turned to stare at her, at once thrilled and confused by her words.

"Go home, drink a lot of wine, and enjoy the freedom of being childless," Shannon said. "While you can."

We made our way out of the hospital and onto the streets. Light, fluffy snow was falling and the air was frigid. The city was calm, almost oddly so. Gone were the ever-present honking horns and the roar of engines, and in their place was a quiet peace that I rarely found here.

But I wasn't in the mood for peaceful. There was too much on my mind, too many questions in need of answers, and a part of me craved the chaos of rush hour traffic.

"Let's walk," Andy said, gesturing in the general direction of our apartment. She held her hand out to me, and I took it. I'd always take it.

Andy was quiet, too. Her long, long hair spilled out of her beanie and her shoulders were drawn up tight to ward off the cold. She stared at the sidewalk and the falling snow, even when I gazed at her for full minutes while we made our way to the North End and up Hanover Street. She knew I was watching, too.

"Quite the night," I said, starved for words. Even the most banal of them.

"Quite," she replied, catching my eye with a quick smile. "Annabelle really is a precious baby. Just adorable."

She turned her face to the sky and snowflakes gathered on

her cheeks, her eyelashes, her lips. I watched those tiny crystals land and melt. Just like the moments passing me by, they were here one second and vapor the next.

"Do you want this?" I asked, running my fingers through my hair. It was damp with snow but I hardly noticed. "All of this? The crazy holiday gatherings and the babies and everything? Do you want it?"

Andy stopped and stepped in front of me, taking my hands in hers. "Why are you asking me this?"

"Because—fuck, Andy," I stammered. "Because I want to be married to you."

Her gaze snapped to mine and her lips parted. "Patrick, you say this as if I don't already know. We've been engaged for thirteen months. What is happening right now?"

"I want to be married to you," I repeated, a bit more impatiently than necessary. "I know I haven't done any of this right. The proposal—"

"When you rolled over in bed one morning and said, 'Would you just marry me already?'"

"Yeah, that wasn't my most eloquent moment," I admitted, shaking my head. "It wasn't what you deserved and—"

"Would you stop it?" Andy paced away from me. "I deserve someone who loves me as I am. Who adores my raw, imperfect form. That's all I need, and it's all I want. I don't know where you got the idea that eloquence was a requirement."

"What about Maine?" I asked, staring while she continued up the street.

"Irrelevant," she called over her shoulder.

"It wasn't irrelevant, Andy," I yelled, my words echoing off the buildings around us. "It was fucking brutal."

She stopped, pivoting to face me. "It *was* brutal. I'll give you that," she conceded, throwing her hands up. "I'm sad. I'm disappointed. I'm confused. My mother said a lot of things that were difficult to hear."

"And you're wondering whether she's right about any of it," I said.

"That's what you think?" she asked, a laugh twisting through her words.

Then she laughed for a full minute. Maybe longer. I wasn't sure because each ripple of laughter hit me like a confusing punch to the gut.

"Help me out, please," I said. "I have no idea what part of this conversation is amusing."

"I needed that," she said, brushing tears from her cheeks. "I don't take my cues on marriage or monogamy from anyone but myself. If I didn't want that with you, if I didn't believe in it, I never would've said yes or accepted this." She held up her gloved left hand and wiggled her ring finger. "Now, tell me what's really going on."

I marched toward her, hating the distance between us, but the ground was slick and I lost my footing. I went down like rhinoceros, a clumsy, fumbling mess. Andy approached me, careful to avoid the iciest patches, and extended her hand. I shuffled to my knees but didn't stand. Not yet.

"I want to grow old with you," I said, staring into her eyes. "I want you to remodel our place because I bought the apartment across the hall, and you're better at reengineering spaces than I am. I want to share every sunset with you, and every sunrise. I want to restore old homes with you. I can't remember how to do it alone anymore. I want to have entire conversations without speaking a single word. I want to let you drive me mad with that goddamn 'hm.' I want to fuck you in dressing rooms, and anywhere else you'll have me. I want to marvel at your knee socks every day. I want to host parties with you because you love them more than I hate them. I want to have a family with you even though that scares the shit out of me. I want to be the best decision you ever made. I want another ring on your finger and one on mine. I want you to be my wife, Andy, and I don't want to wait one more minute."

"Hmmm," she murmured, and it killed me. It killed me because that little sound meant yes, no, maybe, and a million other things, but more than any of that, it meant she wasn't giving me a complete answer when I wanted it the most. She winded her way around thoughts, weaving them together slowly, precisely, and never at the pace I wanted. "You bought the apartment across the hall?"

I blinked up her. "Yes," I said with a fuck-ton of hesitance.

Andy shook some snowflakes from my hair. "That will be a fun project," she said.

"Will that be our only project?" I asked.

She urged me up, her hands gripping my forearms. "Of course not," she said.

"Give me a date, Kitten." I glanced away, barking out a laugh. "I'd suggest we fly to Vegas tonight but I know you want the whole big traditional thing."

"Not necessarily," she said, shaking her head.

I reached for her waist, dragging her against me. "Don't you dare lie to me. I've seen your Pinterest boards."

"When?" she cried. "How?"

"I look at your phone when you're in the bathroom," I confessed. My thumb passed over the band and stone under her glove. "How do you think I picked out this ring?"

"You really need to think about your stalker tendencies. Lingerie shops. Pinterest boards. It's getting out of hand."

I shrugged. "Will taught me that trick."

"That explains a lot," she murmured.

"Let me tell you what matters to me. I want you happy and I want you to be my wife. Everything else is process. I care only about the product."

Andy laughed. "I was expecting a hard sell for Vegas."

"Like I've said ninety-four times tonight, I want to be married to you," I said. "You can have any kind of wedding you'd like. You can also have a flight to Vegas tonight."

Andy tilted her head to the side, her eyes twinkling as a small, secretive smile pulled at her lips. "What if we did both?"

IT WASN'T the worst of times but this sure as shit wasn't the best of times.

In the best column, I was listing the nun's habit I nicked out of a countryside convent last night. No one fucked with nuns. Most people avoided eye contact with them altogether. Bad memories of wooden rulers and forced recitation of multiplication tables. This vestment was keeping me off the radar and doing a sensational job of concealing both my beard and my injuries.

The convent also yielded a pair of granny glasses, tattered scarves, and a small purse loaded with supplies to treat my injuries. Gauze, alcohol swabs, antibacterial ointment, an old bottle of penicillin, a sewing kit, and a pair of needle-nose pliers.

That was where the best column ended.

As far as the worst of times went, getting shot was at the top of the list. There was a bullet lodged in my flank and I'd been bleeding, slow and steady, for hours. A cold sweat covered my body, my heart was wobbling in my chest, and I could only see straight if I squinted. That was fucking unpleasant but my only objective was getting to the port.

I'd spent the night on the run, zigzagging and backtracking to shake the secret police from my tail, and I didn't have the time to dig that son of a bitch out of my soft tissue. There was also the matter of my broken arm and the electrical current burns on my legs but I could manage those. The gunshot wound though, that thing was going to turn septic in a hot minute.

If those issues weren't enough to earn the distinction of Really Fucking Bad, I had a few more lined up. My CIA handlers had no idea where I was. I hadn't seen my partner Veronica in two weeks, and I suspected she was dead or close to it. My local liaisons were dead, both executed in front of me.

A hostile foreign government had discovered that I'd been spying on them for a wee bit of time. The same hostile foreign government was pissed that I didn't fold under their charming interrogation techniques. I could only imagine they regarded my exit from their off-book detention facility—and all the guards I took out in the process—as an unwanted aggravation.

Based on the activity I'd observed as I made my way north toward the Barents Sea, that government had dispatched entire armies to root me out. They intended to find me and make an international example. Regardless of whether they succeeded at nailing my nuts to the wall, they'd also plan some prime-time retaliation.

I went on squinting at the road ahead, breathing slowly and worrying the rosary beads between my fingers to displace some of the pain streaking through my body. If I could get to the port, I could get home.

I walked with purpose, careful to keep my eyes down and my steps confident. I was playing the part of a local, one who wouldn't normally draw the attention of the heavily armed law enforcement agents on every corner.

It wasn't supposed to go down this way. I figured that was how all agents prefaced their debriefs of operations gone bad. I wouldn't know. My operations never went bad.

Until now.

I'd been working this assignment for almost two years. Two years of cohabitation and marital bliss with a *woman*. Even if that woman was also a highly skilled operative, it was one hell of a long-running hetero con. Two years of chipping away at Moscow's society circles, playing the part of the eccentric antiquities dealer who also trafficked in weapons of war. Two years of planting seeds and watching them germinate.

There was no reason for this operation to fall apart weeks before we were due to get out of town. Our work was airtight and the information we'd gathered was solid gold. There were bumps in the road, for sure, but that was the way with every hop. This hop had been one of the good ones. Difficult, exhausting, grueling—but one of the good ones, until I woke up in a dirt-floored dungeon with my hands and feet shackled to an ancient stone wall.

I stifled a laugh at that. My father liked to say that if you thought an operation was going well, you weren't paying attention.

I had paid attention. I knew this operation, every corner and seam of it.

If I made it home, I was certain he'd tell me I hadn't.

A large family came around the corner, and I spared them a warm glance. "God be with you," I said in Russian, affecting my most provincial accent. Nuns didn't rock the upper-crust city accent I'd employed during my time here.

They nodded, mumbling the blessing back to me. I

hunched into my habit, hoping to obscure some of my height. Nuns weren't six-three.

My thumb and forefinger rolled to another bead as the pain of bone-on-bone radiated up my arm and into my shoulder. I was furious about that. The motherfucker who broke it didn't know what the hell he was doing. He just wailed on me with a lead pipe as if that was going to yield any actionable information. Talk about amateur hour. I needed the use of both arms right now, and I didn't have it because some foot soldier with anger issues didn't like it when I told him his mother was bad in bed.

I pressed the pad of my thumb into a rosary bead as a gust of nausea threatened to knock me over. I continued walking, my gaze trained on the stories-high cargo ships and cranes looming tall over Kola Bay. I was almost there, and breathed a small sigh of relief.

A liquefied natural gas tanker was leaving from Murmansk this morning, one with a crew that knew how to look the other way for the right price. The tanker was set to sail around Scandinavia to the Atlantic, and make several stops along the east coast of North America. If I could get on that tanker, I could send word to my handlers. They needed to pull their operatives out of the country and turn down the volume on current assignments, and prepare for the disproportionate response headed their way.

I picked up my pace as I marched through the rows and lanes of shipping containers. Unsurprisingly, I was the only nun in sight, a spectacle in a sea of metal and machinery. The roughnecks and longshoremen eyed me as I passed, and I offered the sign of the cross in response. Something about that gesture, coupled with my rosary beads and exaggerated hunch, earned tolerant nods from the men.

When I reached the far edge of the port, I lifted my arm in greeting to the quartermaster. He eyed me with an appropriate amount of suspicion as I moved toward him. From the habit's deep pockets, I retrieved a small coin purse. It was lined with enough cash to ensure passage to North America, and a little more to keep the questions at a minimum.

No, I hadn't robbed the convent. Even spies had standards. Most of the cash was courtesy of the secret police I took down on my way out of their black site last night. At the off chance the bills were tagged and traceable, I turned them over in small towns throughout the region. Now, all the money was clean and I was a matter of steps away from surviving the worst of this ordeal.

"A beautiful day the Lord has granted us," I said to him, that provincial accent heavier than ever. I worried my beads, forcing his attention there rather than my face. "Do you have room for one more?"

He regarded me for a long minute in which I debated whether I could strangle him without arousing the notice of the other dockworkers and then stow away aboard the tanker. The short answer was yes, I *could* do that, but no, it wasn't a wise move.

"Room," he repeated, pulling the beanie from his head and wiping his hands on the wool. "Headed for America, you know. I have space for one more on deck five, but only deck five. Nothing less."

In other words, he wanted at least five thousand American dollars.

I held out the coin purse. "You're a true servant of our heavenly Father, my child." If I hadn't been holding back a roar of pain, I would've laughed at myself. I figured I'd laugh later, when a steady stream of morphine was coursing through my veins and my humerus bone wasn't trying to tear through my skin. I'd laugh about this whole fucking thing.

Thankfully, the quartermaster wasn't listening to a word I said. He was concerned only with thumbing through the money. He mouthed the numbers as he counted his head bobbing as he neared five thousand. His eyes lit up when he hit six, and then popped right out of his greedy skull when he closed in on seven.

Every payoff was associated with a moment, a beat where the deal could progress as planned or everything could go pear-shaped. This was that moment. The quartermaster was gripping the cash and sizing me up, debating whether he could shake me down or hold me hostage for more. If I knew his type, I knew he was also thinking about dragging a blade across my throat and throwing me overboard once we left port.

And there was nothing I could do about it. Couldn't reason my way around it. Couldn't walk away. I had to wait it out.

He gestured to the medallions hanging from the rosary beads. "Saint Nicholas," he said, pinching one of the charms between his grubby fingers. "Watches over the seafarers, yeah?"

"The seafarers, yes, of course," I replied. I shook the beads at him. "I've been calling upon Saint Nicholas for safe passage."

He unzipped his coat and peeled back several layers of thermal shirts to reveal his bare chest. He pointed to an old tattoo. "Saint Nicholas." He tipped his head to the gangplank. "Be well, Sister."

I offered him a grateful smile and started up the ramp.

Now, I only needed to survive the rest of this journey. I was one step closer but still an ocean away from the other side of this mission. If I made it home, I was taking a long-ass vacation. I was due for some sun, sand, and a sexy man.

"If," I murmured to myself, laughing as much as my broken body would allow. "I'm getting home if I have to steer this motherfucker myself."

THANK YOU FOR READING! *I hope you enjoyed this holiday visit with the Walsh family. If you're ready for more of Wes and his adventure, check out Missing In Action, now available.*

IF YOU LOVED THE WALSHES, *you're going to adore Talbott's Cove. Meet Brooke and JJ in Far Cry, Annette and Jackson in Hard Pressed, Cole and Owen in Fresh Catch, both available now. Turn the page for an excerpts from Talbott's Cove.*

JOIN *my newsletter for news and updates, as well new release alerts, exclusive extended epilogues and bonus scenes, and more.*

IF NEWSLETTERS AREN'T *your thing, follow me on BookBub for preorder and new release alerts.*

VISIT MY PRIVATE READER GROUP, *Kate Canterbary's Tales, for exclusive giveaways, sneak previews of upcoming releases, and book talk.*

also by kate canterbary

Vital Signs

Before Girl — Cal and Stella

The Worst Guy — Sebastian Stremmel and Sara Shapiro

The Walsh Series

Underneath It All – Matt and Lauren

The Space Between – Patrick and Andy

Necessary Restorations – Sam and Tiel

The Cornerstone – Shannon and Will

Restored — Sam and Tiel

The Spire — Erin and Nick

Preservation — Riley and Alexandra

Thresholds — The Walsh Family

Foundations — Matt and Lauren

The Santillian Triplets

The Magnolia Chronicles — Magnolia

Boss in the Bedsheets — Ash and Zelda

The Belle and the Beard — Linden and Jasper-Anne

Talbott's Cove

Fresh Catch — Owen and Cole

Hard Pressed — Jackson and Annette

Far Cry — Brooke and JJ

Rough Sketch — Gus and Neera

Benchmarks Series

Professional Development — Drew and Tara

Orientation — Jory and Max

Brothers In Arms

Missing In Action — Wes and Tom

Coastal Elite — Jordan and April

Get exclusive sneak previews of upcoming releases through Kate's newsletter and private reader group, The Canterbary Tales, on Facebook.

about kate

USA Today Bestseller Kate Canterbary writes smart, steamy contemporary romances loaded with heat, heart, and happy ever afters. Kate lives on the New England coast with her husband and daughter.

You can find Kate at www.katecanterbary.com

facebook.com/kcanterbary

twitter.com/kcanterbary

instagram.com/katecanterbary

amazon.com/Kate-Canterbary

bookbub.com/authors/kate-canterbary

goodreads.com/Kate_Canterbary

pinterest.com/katecanterbary

tiktok.com/@katecanterbary

Acknowledgments

The Walshes wouldn't have come this far without the readers who love them. Thank you to the smart, sassy, pervy members of The Canterbary Tales group. This one is all for you.

I wouldn't have come this far without my husband's support.

www.ingramcontent.com/pod-product-compliance
Lightning Source LLC
Chambersburg PA
CBHW021330190726
48288CB00003B/1036